A RIFLE BARREL APPEARED OVER THE RIM OF THE MESA.

That was the first thing Joe saw. The first thing Chee Two Hats saw as he rode over the rim of the mesa with his two Indian companions was Joe Howard crouching behind a Gatling gun aimed directly at them.

"What do you want?" Joe asked.

"We come for guns," Chee Two Hats replied pointing to the Gatling. "I had agreement with other white men. You come and take. Guns are mine. Not yours."

"The guns aren't mine to give," Joe replied resolutely.

The Indian's stolid brown face changed expression, if a minute twitch of the thin mouth could be called a change, but an instant later the Indians were jerking Henry rifles up to their shoulders.

Joe bent over, hoping he was doing the right thing, and began turning the Gatling crank as fast as he could.

A sound which he'd heard only once before echoed across the mountains and desert. Five seconds later, Joe stared in disbelief at the ground in front of him. . . .

POWELL'S ARMY
BY TERENCE DUNCAN

#1: UNCHAINED LIGHTNING (1994, $2.50)
Thundering out of the past, a trio of deadly enforcers dispenses its own brand of frontier justice throughout the untamed American West! Two men and one woman, they are the U.S. Army's most lethal secret weapon—they are POWELL'S ARMY!

#2: APACHE RAIDERS (2073, $2.50)
The disappearance of seventeen Apache maidens brings tribal unrest to the violent breaking point. To prevent an explosion of bloodshed, Powell's Army races through a nightmare world south of the border—and into the deadly clutches of a vicious band of Mexican flesh merchants!

#3: MUSTANG WARRIORS (2171, $2.50)
Someone is selling cavalry guns and horses to the Comanche—and that spells trouble for the bluecoats' campaign against Chief Quanah Parker's bloodthirsty Kwahadi warriors. But Powell's Army are no strangers to trouble. When the showdown comes, they'll be ready—and someone is going to die!

#4: ROBBERS ROOST (2285, $2.50)
After hijacking an army payroll wagon and killing the troopers riding guard, Three-Fingered Jack and his gang high-tail it into Virginia City to spend their ill-gotten gains. But Powell's Army plans to apprehend the murderous hardcases before the local vigilantes do—to make sure that Jack and his slimy band stretch hemp the legal way!

Available wherever paperbacks are sold, or order direct from the Publisher. Send cover price plus 50¢ per copy for mailing and handling to Zebra Books, Dept. 2925, 475 Park Avenue South, New York, N.Y. 10016. Residents of New York, New Jersey and Pennsylvania must include sales tax. DO NOT SEND CASH.

TWO GUNS FROM TEXAS

ERLE ADKINS

ZEBRA BOOKS
KENSINGTON PUBLISHING CORP.

ZEBRA BOOKS

are published by

Kensington Publishing Corp.
475 Park Avenue South
New York, NY 10016

First printing: March, 1990

Printed in the United States of America

Chapter I

The stone walls and gates at Fort Davis, Texas were a welcome sight as Joe Howard topped a hill and looked down. The fort was surrounded by tall granite mountains. He'd never seen it look so good.

"Sarge, if we can just get past McRaney's office without him seeing us," Joe said out loud to the seal-black horse under him, "you can get a good rub down, some hay and oats and I can get a bath and go to sleep." His shoulders slumped and he could hardly hold his eyes open. The big horse rumbled low in his throat as if he understood every word Joe said to him.

The ride from Fort Stockton had been long and hot and he was bone tired, hungry, and dirty. More tired than hungry though. Too bad a man's destiny couldn't be controlled by his desires. The words had no more than left Joe's mouth when he heard a deep barrel sounding voice call out to him. He'd hoped to miss McRaney, sneak into the barracks and go to sleep. The bath could wait.

"Hey, Joe." Joe turned around, although he didn't have to, to really know who was calling him. The tall colonel beckoned to him with a wave of his long arm. "Tie that black nag of yours up and come here."

Joe looked across the distance and something in the back of his mind told him that the black stage-coach in front of the guest quarters and the two canvas covered wagons in front of the barracks would play an important part in the reason McRaney wanted to see him.

Joe expelled a deep disappointed breath and let his shoulders droop in fatigue, and yes, in irritation. *McRaney thinks I can do the work of two men. The only bad thing about it, I'm only getting the pay of one man.*

"Can I get a drink of water first?" Joe yelled back as he dismounted. In spite of his irked feelings he chuckled when McRaney nodded.

Joe led Sarge on to the corral, unsaddled him then drew a bucket of water from the well by the gate. From a tin dipper he took a long cool drink. The water tasted sweet and quenched his thirst. A thought struck him. He took his hat off and poured a dipper full over his head. The water was invigorating as it trickled over his face, down his neck and chest. Pushing his wet light brown hair carelessly back out of his face, he clamped his battered black flat-crowned hat on and kicked through the loose dust toward McRaney's office.

"If I hurry and get this over," Joe muttered out loud to himself, stomping up the three short steps, "the sooner I can get to sleep. I just hope my eyes stay open long enough."

Eric McRaney was sitting behind a neatly arranged desk when Joe opened the door and went into the office. It was as austerely arranged as the desk. A Rebel flag hung on one wall over a black safe and an American flag hung at the other end of the office. A rack of deer antlers with eight points hung on the wall by the door for a hat rack. McRaney still enjoyed telling about how he'd gotten it four years ago.

Joe felt like a tramp in comparison to the way McRaney looked. The colonel's dark blue shirt and blue pants with a gold stripe down the side fitted his tall, thin frame well. His black hair was combed back neatly and his black beard closely trimmed.

"Joe, I've got a job for you that will thrill you green," McRaney said, grinning slyly up at Joe. "Sit down and I'll tell you all about it."

Joe sat down in a straight-backed chair and tilted it back against the wall.

McRaney's slate-blue eyes twinkled and Joe's heart sank down into his scuffed black boots. He'd come to realize long ago that when McRaney's eyes had that devilish gleam in them, he was in for something that could end up being dangerous and not at all thrilling.

"Well, do I have to wait until Christmas to find out what it is?" Joe said cryptically, crossing his long legs and drawing his mouth into a thin line.

"Mrs. Dorthea Claxton and her son, Harlon, are here from San Antonio," McRaney began, leaning back in a well-oiled swivel chair. He put his elbows on the arm rests, peaked his long finger tips together and peered intently over them at Joe.

"I guess that explains the stagecoach," Joe said, taking a deep breath. "That means someone is going somewhere and needs a guide."

"You guessed right," McRaney said, nodding slowly and pursing his mouth. "Now, I suppose you want to know where you fit in." He arched his thin black brows and inclined his head toward Joe.

"It would help a little," Joe replied, lowering his head and narrowing his eyes.

McRaney stood up slowly and walked in long easy strides over to the window through which the towering Davis Mountains could be seen. Turning around, he sat down on the wide sill and faced Joe.

"Major Edward Claxton, the commandant at the fort in Las Cruces, New Mexico bought two wagon loads of Henry repeating rifles in San Antonio," McRaney said, folding his arms across his chest. "Something about some Indians came up and he had to hurry back. That left his wife and son to bring them."

"Where did Claxton buy so many guns?" Joe asked, his skin beginning to crawl. Two wagons full of guns were a lot to be transporting. And Henry repeating rifles would be an added bonus. If they fell into the wrong hands anything could happen. The narrowed gleam in McRaney's eyes told Joe that it wouldn't be long before he dropped the other boot.

"He bought them in San Antonio from a man from New Orleans," McRaney answered, getting up and walking back to his desk. "Mrs. Claxton needs a guide from here to Las Cruces."

Here it comes, Joe told himself with an inward smile. Please let the roof fall in before he tells me, Joe prayed, looking up toward the bare raftered ceiling. Joe knew he'd be the guide but he wasn't going to volunteer to go. He knew McRaney would enjoy filling him in on all of the details.

"I told Mrs. Claxton that you'd be back today," McRaney went on, cocking his brow and smiling cunningly at Joe. "You've been out in that part of the country before and shouldn't have any problems."

A short silence hung over the office as Joe listened for the ceiling to start cracking. Destiny could still save him from this. But that didn't happen.

"Oh, Eric, come on," Joe cajoled, a frown on his forehead and a pleading in his eyes and voice. "If they got this far without someone holding their hands, why do they need a guide now?"

Joe had never been around children all that much and in his mind's eye he could see a smart-mouthed little brat with a bowl-type hat on his head and wearing short pants. Dorthea Claxton would probably turn out to be a skinny black haired old witch!

Part of his assumption would come true.

"Well," McRaney drew out, slapping his hands down against his legs and standing up, "they made it with a lot of luck and the fact that there aren't too many unpatrolled miles between here and San Antonio. Most of the Indian trouble is in Arizona and Northern New Mexico right now. You are a good scout and that's why I want you to go along with them."

"What if I hadn't come back today?" Joe asked, crossing his right leg over the left knee. "What would you have done?"

McRaney smiled shrewdly down at Joe. "I would have extended the widely publicized hospitality of Fort Davis to them until you arrived."

Joe roared in laughter as he wondered why things always sounded so simple when McRaney explained them to him, and then had a way of turning into disaster when reality finally set in.

"If I sit here long enough," Joe said, squinting his eyes up at McRaney and drawing his mouth in against his teeth, "you'll tell me that I'm sleeping; that's where I want to be, and am having a bad dream."

Joe stood up and McRaney shook his head when a knock sounded at the door. McRaney called out, the door banged open, and a woman who was far from

Joe's idea of Mrs. Dorthea Claxton came charging in.

Joe stood five feet and seven inches tall and was a little on the thin side, weighing about a hundred and twenty pounds. Dorthea Claxton looked at him at almost eye level with green haughty eyes. She had at least twenty pounds on him and the bright blue muslin dress she wore only made her look that much bigger.

Red hair that couldn't have come from anywhere but a bottle of titian was pinned up in large curls over which a floppy brimmed hat was perched at an arrogant angle. Her thin lips were pressed into a tight line and her reddish brown brows arched over her eyes. Her cheeks were vivid with red rouge.

Joe closed his eyes and shook his head in a quick jerk. I can just imagine what her kid looks like. He must have grinned without knowing it.

"Wipe that insidious smile off your face," she snapped contemptuously in a high pitched voice. Joe opened his eyes at the crack of her voice and saw her glance from him over to McRaney. "Is this what I've been waiting for?" she asked, looking Joe up and down. Her mouth curled into a snarl like she was smelling a piece of rotten meat. His appearance wasn't conducive to her personal safety. His blue pants were faded and a little tattered around the cuffs and pockets. The light blue shirt was sweat-stained under the arms and around the neck and dirty. His comfortable boots were scuffed and dusty and his flat-crowned black hat had seen many miles. Her eyes narrowed as she turned back toward McRaney.

"Mrs. Claxton, this is Joe Howard," McRaney introduced, after clearing his throat. "Joe, this is Mrs. Dorthea Claxton. Where's Harlon?"

"I am Mrs. Major Dorthea Claxton to you and anybody else," she corrected sarcastically, tossing her head, "and Harlon is resting."

Joe turned slowly, lowered his head and looked at McRaney. Apparently McRaney knew what Joe was thinking because he shook his head just enough for Joe to notice. Joe turned back toward the woman who was falling into the witch category again.

"This man looks like he couldn't lead a cow to a barn," she said contemptuously, distaste in her voice. "Are you sure he's the best you have for a job like this?"

McRaney stood up and started to say something in Joe's defense. But Joe didn't need anyone to take his side in anything. He could defend himself and he wasn't about to let this old biddy insult him like this.

"Mrs. Claxton," he said slowly, omitting her self administered title, a small knot working in his right jaw, "I can lead a gnat through the eye of a needle. I can take a fly off your hat with a knife and you will never know it. I can pull a snake through your hair without it biting you." His voice was harsh and his breath came in short gasps. "I'm the best at what I do."

A coldness settled over Joe and he knew he was in for the experience of his life in taking this pompous woman and her son to Las Cruces. But he knew he wouldn't miss it for the world. Wonder if the son is anything like his mother? Maybe he lucked out and took after his father. The little tyke must be worn completely out to be resting in the middle of such a hot day. Joe and Mrs. Claxton stared at each other. The hostility was thick enough between the two to cut with a dull knife.

"Mrs. Claxton," McRaney began, a light smile on his bearded face, "Joe is . . ."

"I am Mrs. Major Dorthea Claxton," she corrected, whirling around to glare at McRaney, plopping her hands on her ample hips. "That's how I want to be addressed by you and everybody else, and don't forget it."

"All right," McRaney agreed conciliatorily, drawing out the words. He stared down at the desk and chewed on his under lip for a few seconds. He seemed to be trying not to laugh at the woman and keep control of himself at the same time.

"Joe knows what he's doing," McRaney went on, looking up at her. "This isn't his first job. He's one of the best scouts I've ever known."

"I'm taking you at your word, Colonel McRaney," Dorthea Claxton snapped, her green eyes flashing. "I want to leave early tomorrow morning." She turned and started to leave the room which was beginning to close in on Joe.

"Wait just a minute," Joe called out, irritation edging his voice. "There are a few things I need to know before we start out on this joy ride. Who drives the stage? Who drives the two wagons? Are we going to have any kind of escort or is it just the three of us?"

His eyes burned from lack of sleep and his stomach pulled into a bitter knot. Some food would help. He hadn't liked Mrs. Major Dorthea Claxton from the minute he'd laid eyes on her. He knew it was going to be a long way to Las Cruces and there were a few things he needed to know.

"My son and I drove the stage," she answered, turning back around to face him and expelling a disgruntled breath. "W.C. Bassett drove one of the wagons and we'll have to get another driver. Before you ask about that, the other driver didn't want to go any farther than here. He wanted to go back to

San Antonio. He didn't feel safe here." Sarcasm was in her voice and she pulled her mouth down.

Joe felt a grin pulling at his mouth but struggled to hold his lips straight. The man probably didn't feel safe with her along or couldn't stand her mouth any longer. She'd probably talk him to death.

"Harlon and I will see you early in the morning, Mr. Howard," she said crisply, lifting her head and snapping her eyes. "Getting those guns to my husband at the fort as soon as possible is very important." She opened and slammed the door shut behind her.

"Thanks a lot, Eric," Joe said sarcastically, tilting his head to one side. "I'll make you a deal: why don't you take Mrs. Major Dorthea Claxton and her kid to New Mexico and I'll stay here and run the fort."

McRaney sat down on the edge of the desk again, slowly opened and closed his eyes. He took a slow breath and let it hiss out through his teeth. Shaking his head lazily, he drew his mouth into a thin line. "Now, Joe," he said pragmatically, a gleam coming back into his blue eyes, "you know there's nothing in the world you'd rather do than escort Mrs. Major Dorthea Claxton and Harlon to New Mexico." McRaney's voice was flat.

Joe knew he was going on the trip but he actually enjoyed playing this little cat and mouse game with McRaney.

"Okay, you win," Joe said, expelling a deep breath and pulling his hat down on his forehead. "Why don't we go check the wagons? I think I should see what's in them, don't you?"

"You go ahead," McRaney said, sitting down behind the desk and picking up a pen and making a notation on a piece of paper. "I checked one of the wagons when they came in last night."

"All right," Joe said, opening the door. "If there's nothing else surprising that you want to tell me, I'm going to check the wagons and then take a bath." He pulled the front of his blue shirt away from his chest and curled his lips in a snarl. "Whew," he said, shaking his head in several small jerks. "I'll see you at supper."

Joe started toward the two wagons in front of the barracks but his need for a bath overpowered his curiosity about the guns and he hurried on to the barracks.

Taking clean clothes and a bar of soap from a trunk under his bed, Joe walked in long strides about a hundred yards from the fort to a pond. He could have used the bath house behind the barracks but he wanted a quiet bath. Something in the back of his mind told him that this would be his last chance for such a bath in a long time and he wanted to enjoy it.

Joe undressed and waded out in the cool water until it was a little over his knees. Splashing water over his lean body, he lathered up thickly then eased down in the water and breathed a relaxing sigh as the dirt and sweaty smell floated away with the soap. Running the soap bar over his face and head he lay back in the water, submerging himself. He stayed under until his lungs began burning for air, and he stood up.

Joe was pushing his dripping hair back out of his face when suddenly cold chills, which had nothing to do with a warm breeze blowing on his wet body, raced up and down his back. Goose bumps stood up on his arms and he shivered. He felt eyes probing into him and knew without a doubt that he was being watched. But by whom? And why? Did this have anything to do with Dorthea Claxton, her son

Harlon and the guns?

Walking out of the water, he quickly pulled on his pants and picked up the gun belt and strapped it around his waist. Dropping down on one knee and in the pretense of looking into his boot for crawly things, he looked behind him, where he expected to see someone standing. But he didn't see anyone. From past experience, though, he knew he hadn't been wrong.

Was someone from the fort waiting for the seclusion of the pond for a bath like he'd done? That didn't make sense. The pond was large enough for at least twenty people to bathe in it without anyone knowing they were there.

Maybe it was some animal. No, he quickly refuted, shaking his head and pulling on his socks and boots. The biggest mountain lion in the Davis Mountains wouldn't have given him a feeling like this.

Whoever was watching him had to know that he'd just gotten back to the fort. Had they followed him from Fort Stockton? No, that was stupid! Why would anyone want to do that? What would be the purpose and what would be gained from it?

Could this be connected in some way to the guns in the two wagons in front of the barracks, he asked himself again? He decided to have another talk with Mrs. Major Dorthea Claxton as soon as he got back to the fort. The bath had made him feel much better and he could cope with the old battle axe again. Putting on his shirt and hat, he started back.

The uneasy feeling vanished as he walked through the back gate at the fort. Dropping his dirty clothes off at the wash house, he started toward the guest quarters.

"Yoo hoo, Mr. Howard," he heard called out, and

he stopped in his tracks. He didn't have to look around to know who it was. The woman's voice sounded like a chicken trying to cackle with a string tied around its neck. Slowly he turned around to see Mrs. Major Dorthea Claxton bustling toward him. She was coming from the tack shed. Joe wanted to laugh so bad he could hardly stand it.

She had changed from her floppy hat to a poke bonnet. The ribbons weren't tied and the ends of them flapped in the breeze, giving the impression that she was on the verge of flying. Joe shook his head and waited for her to catch up with him.

"I was just on my way to see you, ma'am," he said, swallowing hard. He drew his mouth in against his teeth so he wouldn't laugh. He wondered what she was doing at the tack shed. He felt sorry for Boss Owens, the old soldier who did all of the leather mending.

"What would you possibly want to see me about?" she asked cryptically, looking him up and down. "You look like a different person now that you're clean," she went on bluntly before he could answer her question. "That's one thing I've insisted on since we've been traveling; taking a bath at least every two days. I hope you'll remember it."

Joe couldn't stop his brows from whipping up over his surprised eyes. How in the world did this woman expect to take a bath out in the middle of nowhere every other day? But right now something told him not to argue with her. He just nodded his head.

"What did you want to see me about?" she asked again and began walking in strides that almost matched his toward the stagecoach.

"Did you happen to notice anyone following you after you left San Antonio?" Joe asked, hooking his thumbs in the belt loops. He felt silly asking the question. Surely no one like Mrs. Major Dorthea Claxton would be that observant. But he was to get another of many surprises from this obstinate woman standing before him with a perplexed look on her highly rouged face.

"Strange that you should ask such a thing," she answered, drawing her brows together and batting her eyes rapidly. "I was sure someone had been following us all day just before we got to the fort. Harlon and Mr. Bassett didn't seem to agree with me. But George O'Mally, that was the other driver, thought there was someone out there. Why do you ask?" She lowered her head and looked up at him, the frown still on her face, pulling three deep lines between her thinly arched brows.

When Joe had finished telling her about the incident at the pond, he was sure he saw her shiver. Her huge bosom expanded as she took a deep breath and her haughtiness seemed to ebb a degree as she expelled it.

"If someone is following you," Joe began, pulling his mouth to one side, knowing what the answer would be before he asked it, "do you suppose it would have anything to do with the guns?"

Maybe the man from New Orleans wanted them back. But why would he be following Joe? He should have been at the fort watching Mrs. Claxton and her son.

She stared up at him for a long time then slowly lowered her eyes and looked down at her black high buttoned shoes. Hesitantly she looked up at him again. She appeared to shrink a few inches.

"Yes, I would guess that it could be something connected with the guns," she finally answered.

"Mrs. Claxton," Joe began and stopped when he saw her stiffen her shoulders. "Mrs. Major Claxton," he began again and rolled his eyes toward the sky when he watched her relax. He realized that she would only be addressed the last way. "Are you telling me everything about those guns? Are you hiding something from me? If you are, you'd better tell me now! It could make all the difference in the world in us getting killed between here and New Mexico."

Mrs. Major Dorthea Claxton drew herself up to her usual confident height once more and glared at him.

"I've told you all you need to know about those guns," she snapped, plopping her hands on her hips again. "It's going to be your job getting them, Harlon and me to the fort at Las Cruces."

She started to turn toward the white cottage guests used, but Joe stopped her. "Just when do I get to meet Harlon?" he asked, facing her. "And what were you going to ask me just then?"

"In the morning will be soon enough for you to meet Harlon," she answered cryptically. "I wanted to know if you've thought of another driver?" Before he could answer and in a swirl of her blue skirt she flounced inside the house and slammed the door shut behind her.

This time Joe's curiosity couldn't be ignored. He turned and in swift strides went to the narrow lead wagon in front of the barracks. Untying the canvas top, he flung it all the way back. He wasn't ready for what his eyes saw. Only one box about three feet tall was strapped and tied to each side of the wagon with thin ropes. Joe had just untied the rope and was using the butt of the long barreled Colt .45 to loosen the top of the box when he heard a man yell at him.

"Hey, you!" The voice was deep and sullen. "What do you think you're doing to that box?"

Joe looked up only long enough to see a tall man coming from the barracks. He wore a light tan shirt, brown pants and a Remington .44 was strapped around his waist. A gray oval-crowned hat sat squarely on his head.

"I asked you a question," the man reminded. Joe looked up for a second. The man's hand was resting on the pistol grip. Joe guessed from the low angle the pistol rode on the man's thin hips that he knew how to use it. Joe knew he'd better explain his actions and quick.

"I'm Joe Howard," he said and extended his right hand in what he hoped was a friendly enough gesture. "I'm the scout here at Fort Davis and I've been volunteered to take a crazy woman and her kid to the fort at Las Cruces, New Mexico. Now," he went on in the same smooth voice and looking steadily into the man's blue eyes, "who are you?"

Joe wasn't ready for the deep laugh that burst from the man's throat. The man actually threw back his head and roared in laughter until tears glistened in his eyes. Finally he regained his composure, cleared his throat and coughed.

"I'm W. C. Bassett," he said, taking Joe's hand in a firm grip. "I drove that wagon," he nodded his head toward the one they were standing beside. "All the way from San Antonio. I guess I'll go the rest of the way with you. But we need another driver. Are you it?"

"Nooo," Joe said, shaking his head and frowning at Bassett. "I'm just going along as a guide. I don't really understand why you need one since you got this far without one."

Bassett started to laugh again but took a deep breath and didn't. "As we go along you'll realize that it doesn't do any good to argue with Mrs. Major

Dorthea Claxton," Bassett said, making a sucking sound with his lips against his teeth. "It's her idea."

Joe couldn't help noticing the sarcasm in Bassett's voice and he couldn't help wondering why he'd laughed so hard when he'd told him who he was and what he'd been hired to do. "What was so funny just then?" Joe had to ask.

The question set Bassett off again. When he'd calmed down, he cleared his throat. "You called her crazy," he reminded, nodding slowly. "That's the best description anybody could give her and it's apparent that you haven't met Harlon yet. I feel sorry for him. Not only is he out here with his mother, he's . . ."

Bassett's statement was cut off by the cook clanging on the iron triangle outside the mess hall.

"You go ahead," Bassett said, giving Joe a soft push on the shoulder. "I'll close this up and be along in a few minutes."

If Joe hadn't been so hungry, he'd have gone ahead and checked the box as he should have done. But he hadn't eaten since early that morning and his stomach was making noises that couldn't be ignored any longer. Deep down he knew he was doing the wrong thing by not looking into the box now but he was sure that there would be enough time before they left tomorrow morning. They still had to get another driver before they could leave.

Joe was so hungry that he hardly tasted the rare venison steak, mashed potatoes, biscuits, and gravy. The only thing that actually registered on his palate was the strong black coffee. He washed down his meal with two cups full and polished off a piece of apple pie with a third. He was sure he'd live until breakfast and left the long, hot and crowded mess hall. Bassett never did come in.

The sun was slipping down behind the looming

Davis Mountains and painting the western sky red and gold. Soon a cool breeze would alleviate the blistering heat that had beat down ruthlessly on the land all day. It would be dark soon and too late to look at the guns tonight. Besides there were other things that needed some attention.

Since Mrs. Dor . . . No, Mrs. Major Dorthea Claxton had voiced a preference for a bath at least every other day, he'd have to see about enough water to last until the next water hole. He remembered four water barrels in the tack shed and headed in that direction. Maybe that's where she'd been when he'd seen her earlier. He opened the door on rusty hinges and went inside.

"Who's there?" A flat voice called out from a room in the back.

"Boss Owens, it's me, Joe Howard." Joe heard a door open and close way in the back. It wasn't long before he heard shuffling footsteps and saw a lantern light coming toward him.

"What kin I do fer ye at this hour?" Owens asked, squinting down at Joe in the dim light. The old man was almost six feet tall and out-weighed Joe by thirty pounds. "I wus jest about to shut my eyes. It's been a long hot day and I'm plumb tuckered."

"Yeah, I know what you mean," Joe agreed, slapping the old man on the shoulder. He had to reach up a little to do it. "This won't take very long. I need to use those four water barrels in the back."

"Four water barrels?" Owens repeated, frowning down at Joe and pulling a suspender up over his red undershirt. "Why do ye need so much water at one time?"

In as few words as possible, because time was wasting and there were a couple of other things to be done, Joe explained to Owens his reason.

"Yer joshin'," Owens refuted, grinning at Joe. "Nobody bathes that often when travelin' like that." From the close sweaty scent of the old trooper Joe didn't think he bathed that often when he wasn't traveling.

"That just goes to show that you haven't met Mrs. Major Dorthea Claxton yet," Joe told him, shaking his head and wrinkling up his forehead. "Didn't you see her earlier? She came over here."

"Is all that her name?" Owens asked, shaking his head and beckoning to Joe to follow him to the back of the tack shed.

"Yeah," Joe told him as they rolled the four barrels out of the shed and over to the well by the corral. Joe told him that he'd fill them in the morning so the water would be that much fresher.

So, with more trepidation than courage or knowledge, Joe Howard became scout for Mrs. Major Dorthea Claxton and her son Harlon.

Joe went to bed worrying about the guns and wondering about the boy. Usually kids made a nuisance of themselves, running around and getting into everything in new surroundings. But there had been no sign of Harlon Claxton. Maybe his mother had him tied to the bed!

He worried about what else there was about the guns that neither the major's wife nor W. C. Bassett wanted him to know. All of that would be found out in due time, Joe told himself as he undressed down to his shorts and went to bed.

Around midnight he was awakened from a sound sleep by someone trying to tiptoe across the barracks floor. At first he didn't think anything about it. The troops were constantly getting up to go outside to the latrine. But there was something strange about the man moving slowly across the wooden floor.

Joe raised up on one elbow. There was just enough moonlight coming in through the open window for him to make out W. C. Bassett. It dawned on Joe that the strange thing about Bassett was that he was fully dressed; right down to his hat and gun. If he'd only been going to answer nature's call he'd have had on no more than his pants and boots.

Had Bassett heard something at the wagons? Joe wondered, giving the tall man the benefit of a doubt. Was he going out to check on the guns? Consumed with curiosity Joe got up and eased over to the window. He got a double surprise!

Bassett wasn't alone at the wagons. The very last person Joe ever expected to see up at this hour was Mrs. Major Dorthea Claxton! Joe could hear their mumbling voices but couldn't make out any definite words. Something told him he should know what they were talking about.

As fast as he could without making any noise Joe hurried back to his bunk, jerked on his pants and boots. Snatching the Colt .45 from the holster, Joe went out the back door and eased around the end of the barracks. The lead wagon was only a few feet from the end of the building and it was easy for Joe to hear what they were saying.

"No, he didn't look into the box," Bassett was saying. Joe could see him shaking his head in the moonlight.

"Oh, that's good," Dorthea Claxton replied, expelling a deep sigh.

"Why don't you want him, or anyone else for that matter, to know what's in the boxes?" Bassett asked, a puzzled tone in his voice.

"Because the fewer who know what we've actually got in these wagons, the better it will be," she answered slowly. There was certainty in the woman's voice and Joe was positive she believed what she'd just said. But he was just as positive now that he wasn't going to go all the way to Las Cruces, New Mexico without knowing exactly what was under the canvas on both wagons.

With that in mind, Joe stood up and walked purposefully toward the two people at the wagon. Bassett jerked the Remington .44 from the holster and Dorthea Claxton gasped in surprise at Joe's sudden appearance. Joe's assumption about Bassett's ability with the gun was proving true.

"Well, it might not be best for everybody to know what's in those wagons," Joe said bluntly, "but it will certainly be best for me if I know what's in them."

"Mr. Howard," Dorthea Claxton began, "there's really no need to trouble yourself about this." In the moonlight Joe saw her shift her eyes quickly from him over to Bassett.

"Oh, yes, ma'am," he argued, nodding his head slowly and arching his brows. "There is a need for me to trouble myself about what's in those wagons. It could have a great effect on my life."

Joe was already holding the Colt .45 and all he had to do was raise it if Bassett threatened him. But he was greatly relieved when Bassett didn't make a move against him with the gun.

"Now, for my benefit and peace of mind," Joe went on in a level tone, "let's finish what I started just before supper."

Without waiting to see if they'd help or hinder him, Joe untied the rope holding the canvas over the box and threw the cover all the way off.

"Why don't you open it?" Joe suggested, turning to face Bassett. Bassett hesitated for a second then glanced at Dorthea Claxton. It was only after she pulled her mouth into a tight circle and nodded that

Bassett climbed up in the wagon, took the pistol by the barrell and used the butt to take the lid off the box top. There was enough light from the moon for Joe to see something he never expected to run across.

A Gatling gun, instead of Henry repeating rifles took up the whole box! It was the first gun of its type that Joe had ever seen. He'd heard about them and the damage one could do but he couldn't understand why they'd told everybody that they were carrying Henry rifles to New Mexico. What was the reason for the deception. Why only one gun in the box?

"Is this what's in the other box?" he asked pointedly, turning around and squinting his eyes at Dorthea Claxton.

"Yes," she replied haughtily, expelling a deep breath. "I only said we were taking Henry rifles because they wouldn't attract as much attention as a Gatling gun. You can see why for yourself."

"Does Colonel McRaney know about these?" Joe asked, jerking a thumb over his shoulder toward McRaney's office.

"Yes," Dorthea Claxton answered. "He agreed that it would be best if only a few people knew about it."

Hot rage swept over Joe like a fire out of control. Why had Eric McRaney lied to him? He didn't have time to ask him tonight and it probably wouldn't do any good to ask him in the morning. They would be leaving anyway, so what would it prove if he did ask him and if McRaney did tell him what was in the wagons.

"Did the other driver know about these?" Joe asked Bassett. The tall man shook his head, turned and went back into the barracks. "Would you like me to walk you back to the guest cottage?" Joe asked Mrs. Claxton, hoping to see Harlon Claxton.

"No," she snapped, spinning around and stomping off, leaving him there by the wagon. It didn't take long to put the lid back on the box and retie the canvas. By the time Joe got back to the barracks, Bassett had gone to bed and there was nothing left to be said anyway.

When Joe awoke the next morning it was still pitch black outside. The moon had long since gone down, taking the shadows with it and it was at least an hour before sunup. But Mrs. Major Dorthea Claxton had said she wanted to leave early and this was early. The troops were already getting up to start on today's patrol, so there was no use in wasting any more time.

Joe got up, put two changes of clothes in one side of the saddle bag and enough ammunition for the Colt .45 and Winchester rifle in the other saddle bag. He ate a hearty breakfast with the troops in the mess hall and noticed that Bassett was already gone or hadn't come in yet.

When he'd finished eating he filled the water barrels from the well and had Boss Owens help him lift them up into the wagon. He was sure that Dorthea Claxton had already made arrangements for food so there was no need for him to worry about that. He was also going to leave it up to her, Bassett, or McRaney to get another driver. He'd only been hired as a guide.

Joe was surprised to find Sarge already saddled when he reached the corral. Bassett was putting the harness on four brown horses. These, Joe assumed, pulled the stage. Eight other horses, probably four for each wagon were already harnessed by the corral.

"Thanks, Bassett," Joe said, taking Sarge's reins

and picking up the reins of the four horses. "I'll hitch up the stage and you do the wagons." Bassett nodded. Nothing was mentioned about last night.

"Yoo hoo, Mr. Howard," Joe heard his name called as he led the four horses toward the stage in front of the guest cottage. Dorthea Claxton's voice did strange things to his nerves. The sun was beginning to peep over the mountains and there was just enough light to see her.

The brightness of her blue dress of yesterday was rivaled by a bright green this morning. A wide floppy brimmed hat was perched on top of her red hair. "Will you get someone to load our luggage?" she said crisply and pointing to a pile of hat boxes and three trunks by the door. She flounced off toward the mess hall and Joe bent down to pick up a tall hat box.

"I'll help you with that," a man's voice said from behind him. Joe raised up and turned around. He wasn't ready for what he saw. A tall man, at least six feet, two inches, was buttoning up the front of a soft blue shirt. A wide-brimmed white straw hat was pushed back on his angular head. He was very pale and almost skeletal thin. He looked ill and Joe guess that it would take only a mild breath to blow him away. Joe surmised that he was nearer his own age of twenty-three, but looked at least ten years older. His brown eyes were red-rimmed and the sallow skin was stretched over high cheekbones.

"Good morning, Mr. Howard," he continued in a wheezy voice and extended a bony hand. "I'm Harlon Claxton." Looking at him closer, Joe noticed that the shirt hung loosely from his shoulders. There and around the cuffs and waist where the shirt was tucked into dark blue pants was the only place the shirt touched his body. "I hope we can get these guns to my father without too much trouble."

It seemed to take a great deal of effort for Harlon Claxton to get the few words out. He struggled to pull air into his lungs.

If he's this sick, Joe wondered, shaking his cool hand, and there was no doubt that he was, how in the world was he able to drive a stage from San Antonio to here?

"Well, if the Indians and bandits will cooperate," Joe said, grinning then pulling his mouth into a thin line, "we shouldn't have any problems."

For some reason, Joe didn't believe his own words. They would be crossing a land that belonged to another culture who resented their intrusion, as any sensible people would, and there was bound to be trouble and lots of problems.

The trouble would come for certain if the Indians and bandits found out about the kind of guns they were carrying. One gun could fire as many as three hundred rounds of ammunition a minute or as fast as a man's arm could turn the crank. It would be an asset to anybody.

"Is there a driver for the other wagon yet?" Joe asked Claxton as they finished stowing the last hat box in the boot of the stage. Claxton was totally exhausted and leaned against the wheel to get his breath.

"I don't think so," he replied, struggling to take a deep lung full of air and pushing dark brown hair back out of his pale face. "I . . ." He was interrupted when McRaney called out to Joe.

"Now before you start in about the guns," McRaney began, holding up his hand at the accusing look in Joe's eyes and walking up beside the two men, with a sheepish look on his bearded face, "I want you to know that the deception wasn't my idea. It was hers." He nodded toward Dorthea Claxton who was bustling toward them swinging her arms like a windmill late for work.

"Yes, the idea was mine," she admitted cynically, tossing her head and arching her thin brows at them. "I explained the entire reason to Mr. Howard last night. Not that it mattered one way or the other." A defiant gleam narrowed her green eyes.

"What do you mean, didn't matter?" Joe asked hotly, his brown eyes snapping. "We're not going on a picnic, you know."

"Wait a minute," Harlon Claxton said sternly, taking a ragged breath. "Wait a minute." He held up his thin hand to silence them. "Arguing now won't do any good." He started to say something else but his thin frame was wracked by a spasm of hard coughing. Dorthea Claxton reached up and patted his flushed face. She opened the stage door and he sat down on the floor.

"Ma'am, could I speak to you for a minute," Joe asked, touching her arm and indicating away from the stage with his thumb. The look on her face told him she already knew what he wanted to talk about but she nodded and followed him anyway.

"It's beyond me how your son got this far, as sick as he is," Joe said bluntly, frowning at her. "It's a long way to New Mexico and hot and dusty. He won't be able to make it if he has to drive. Have you given any thought to two extra drivers?" Joe thought that a mother's concern for a son who was as obviously ill as Harlon was would have some effect on the woman standing before him. Maybe it would have on an ordinary woman but he'd already learned that Dorthea Claxton was far from being ordinary.

"Harlon can make it by himself," she said shortly, her hands on her hips and digging in her fingers.

"He always coughs like that when he gets up in the morning. One driver will be enough. Have you gotten one yet?"

"Me?" Joe questioned, blinking his eyes a couple of times and frowning. "I'm just supposed to be the guide. I didn't know it was up to me to get the other driver. That should have been your or McRaney's responsibility."

A knot began working in Joe's lean jaw. He was beginning to dislike this heartless woman more and more.

"Just get a driver, Mr. Howard," she snapped, raising her voice, spinning around and going back toward the stage. "Time is wasting."

Joe felt betrayed by McRaney and used by Mrs. Major Dorthea Claxton. Right then he didn't give a tinker's rip if they ever got to Las Cruces. And he really didn't care who they got for a driver.

Looking up he saw Boss Owens standing in the doorway of the tack shed and he grinned deviously when an idea struck him.

"Hey, Boss," he yelled out loudly, walking in long strides across the parade ground, "do you want to drive a wagon to Las Cruces, New Mexico?" If she wanted a driver, he'd get another driver.

When Owens heard his name called he started toward Joe, not sure what he'd said to him. Before Joe could reach Owens, McRaney got to Joe first.

"You don't want Boss Owens to drive that wagon," McRaney said sternly, shaking his head, a frown pulling his black brows tightly together. His eyes snapped and his chiseled nostrils flared in heavy breathing.

"Just why not?" Joe shot back, doubling his hands into fists at his side. "You didn't get a driver. Mrs. Major Dorthea Claxton hasn't gotten a driver and she wants to leave in a few minutes." Sarcasm edged his voice and for the first time since Joe had known McRaney he wanted to hit him so hard he could actually taste it.

"That's beside the point," McRaney argued, shaking his head again as Owens approached them in a trot. "If he leaves here, there won't be anybody to do the tack work."

"Now that's the most stupid thing I've ever heard you say," Joe disputed coldly, closing his eyes slowly and opening them. "What if Boss wanted to take a vacation? He's been here long enough for one. Or, or," he raised his voice when he saw McRaney take a deep breath to interrupt, "or what if he keeled over dead? You'd find somebody!"

Before McRaney could answer or argue with Joe, Owens reached them. He had on the same clothes he'd worn yesterday and probably the day before and a person only escaped the rancid scent of body odor if they were standing well downwind of him. Mrs. Major Dorthea Claxton would really enjoy this! Joe allowed himself an inward vindictive smile. Boss's faded blue shirt with tattered sergeant stripes was wrinkled. The black pants with the baggy legs stuffed down into scuffed black boots looked just as bad. A Colt .44 was strapped around his thin waist.

"What was ye sayin' 'bout New Mexico?" Owens asked in a gruff voice, pushing a dark blue cap back on his head. He spat a long stream of brown tobacco juice in the dust that beaded and quickly disappeared into the dry dust. Excited blue eyes twinkled in his round whiskered face.

"We need another driver for the other wagon," Joe told him, glancing at McRaney, "and I was wondering if you might want to drive it and get away from the fort for a while."

The look in Joe's brown eyes dared the colonel to argue with him. McRaney knew from the set expression on Joe's face and the hot glare in his eyes that Joe was aggravated with the entire matter and just might refuse to go if he was pushed too hard.

"Sure, I guess so," Owens agreed, rubbing his gnarled hands together in anticipation. "When do we leave?" He looked a little surprised when Joe told him in only a few minutes. "Is it okay, Colonel?" McRaney nodded dejectedly. "Jest let me throw some clothes in a sack," Owens said, turning around and starting back toward the tack shed.

"Boss, wait a minute," Joe called out, "come back here." The old man turned around, frowned and retraced his steps, "I'm going to be more truthful with you than some people were with me." Joe threw a castigating look at McRaney. "We're taking Gatling guns to the fort at Las Cruces. Do you still want to go?"

Owens's blue eyes popped wide open and he considered the question for a second. "Sure," he said, shrugging his shoulders, "it wouldn't make no never mind to me if ye was takin' guns to Grant. It's been so long since I've been away from here, I've plumb fergot what it looks like outside them gates."

"Okay," Joe said, nodding with a smile. Owens turned and hurried back toward the tack shed. "Bring a horse for the return trip."

"I hope to God you know what you're doing," McRaney admonished, pulling his mouth into a thin tight line. "He's an old man. A trip like this won't be good for him. He's almost seventy."

Joe shot McRaney a contemptuous look. Something told him that this trip wasn't going to be good for him either. But he didn't have the time to argue the point with McRaney.

By now Bassett had both wagons hitched and was sitting on the spring seat of the lead wagon.

"Are we finally ready?" Mrs. Major Dorthea Claxton called out irritably from inside the stage. Joe turned around and nodded when he saw Owens climb up on the seat of the other wagon.

"Good luck, Joe," McRaney said, extending his hand. "You're going to need it."

Joe wanted to hit McRaney instead of shake hands with him. But he didn't. He just swung up on Sarge and rode toward the gate.

Chapter II

By the time the two wagons and stagecoach rolled through the stone gates of Fort Davis, Texas, the sun had topped the mountains and was telling the travelers that it was going to be another blistering hot day. They had lost almost an hour hitching up the wagons, loading the stage and getting another driver. Joe knew that Mrs. Major Dorthea Claxton wouldn't waste any time in telling him about it when they stopped to rest the horses.

Opportunity presented itself two hours later, more for Harlon Claxton's benefit than the horses though. Claxton hadn't fully recovered from his coughing bout earlier that morning.

Joe had kept glancing back at the pale young man driving the stagecoach. As the stage rocked along it seemed to take every ounce of effort Harlon Claxton had just to stay on the seat and hold the reins in his thin hands. Joe got the impression that the horses were following Bassett's wagon instead of being driven by Claxton.

"He doesn't look so good," Joe mentioned to Bassett, pulling Sarge to a slow walk beside the first wagon. "The horses can go a little farther before they need to rest but he won't make it much longer."

Bassett stood up, turned around and agreed with Joe after a short glance over his shoulder.

"She won't like stopping this soon," Bassett said, arching his brows and shaking his head.

"We don't have any choice," Joe said defiantly. "That man is sick. She's not much of a mother if she puts those guns over her son's health. How long have you known them?"

Bassett sat back down on the spring seat and spat out a stream of tobacco juice. "Not long. Just since San Antonio," he answered, wiping his mouth on the back of his hand. "This isn't the first coughing spell he's had. So far it's the worse though. Are you going to tell her or just stop?"

Joe looked down at the ground, pulled his mouth into a thin line and considered his two options. If he followed Bassett's suggestion it would save him a lot of aggravation. On the other hand if he told Mrs. Major Dorthea Claxton what he wanted to do she'd only argue with him. But she would anyway so why waste time.

Pulling Sarge around, he rode a little away from Bassett's wagon so that Boss Owens could see him. "We're going to stop here for a while," he yelled out and waved his arm in the direction of several cedar trees. The words had no sooner left his mouth when a screeching voice, which could probably be heard all the way over in Mexico called out:

"Yoo hoo, Mr. Howard," she said, leaning over the stage door, the ribbons on her yellow hat fluttering in the breeze, "just why are we stopping so soon? We haven't covered much ground and we have a long way to go. We lost some time this morning, you know."

Something in the woman's voice caused the short hairs on the back of Joe's neck to stand up. Taking a deep breath, he rode over to the stage and glanced up quickly at Harlon Claxton. His thin face was pale and beads of sweat that Joe guessed had nothing to do with the heat, stood out on his forehead.

"Well, ma'am," he said, looking back at her, "the wagons are carrying heavy loads and the horses need a rest." He winced when she flung the stage door open and flounced down the steps. Picking up her green skirt she stomped away from the stage and sat down on a log under a tree.

"Can you make it?" Joe asked, turning back and looking up at Harlon Claxton. He nodded and pulled a ragged breath into his lungs.

Joe dismounted and watched Harlon Claxton climb slowly down from the stage. Bassett and Owens pulled their horses and wagons over by the stage and got down. Joe wanted to offer help to Claxton but knew it would probably embarrass him and his mother would know exactly why they'd stopped so soon.

"Why don't you stretch out in the stage?" Joe asked Claxton when he was standing by him.

"Thanks, I believe I will for a few minutes," Claxton agreed, expelling a deep breath. Joe opened the door for Claxton and got a glimpse inside the stage. It was nothing at all like he expected. He'd ridden in stages before and those had consisted of one seat on either side of the stage. Joe blinked his eyes several times in disbelief. Instead of leather, the seats were covered in a soft shiny blue velvet. The rolled up window flaps were made of the same kind of material but thicker. The floor was covered with a blue and brown rug.

"Mother was never one to travel conventionally," Harlon Claxton said, amusement in his voice. He stepped inside and stretched out on the seat. Joe closed the door and walked slowly toward the disgruntled looking woman sitting on the log.

"Did you really think it was necessary to stop this early?" she asked, glancing up at him. Two irritated lines formed between her green eyes. "If Harlon had to rest, and I'm sure that's why we're here, you could have driven for a while."

Joe couldn't believe how insensitive this woman was. Did getting those Gatling guns to her husband at the fort in New Mexico mean more to her than her son's health? Surely she could see that he was ill.

"Ma'am, I'm not being paid to drive a stagecoach," Joe pointed out shrewdly. "My job is to ride ahead and scout for scalp-taking Indians and money-robbing Mexican bandits." Joe got a good feeling when he saw the pompous woman swallow hard and shivers send goose bumps up and down her arms.

"How many Indians and bandits do you think are around here?" she asked, finally looking around at the looming mountains that seemed to brush the blue sky with their red granite peaks.

"At least four thousand, seven hundred and fifty three," he said dryly and with sarcasm in every word. He gritted his teeth so he wouldn't laugh at her. Boss Owens was standing close enough to hear though and couldn't restrain himself. He jerked his cap off, slammed it down on the ground and doubled over in a fit of laughter. He finally straightened up, cleared his throat and wiped his eyes on the back of his gnarled hand.

"What in the world is the matter with him?" Mrs. Major Dorthea Claxton asked, her eyes wide in astonishment, her mouth gaping open.

"Oh, he's just probably glad to get away from Fort Davis," Joe said, squinting his eyes and pulling his mouth into a thin line. Turning around, Joe went back to Sarge and made a big fuss about checking the black horse's shoes. Boss Owens walked over to Joe and slapped him on the shoulder.

"Ye really put that old windbag in her place, boy," Boss said, probably meaning his words as a compliment. "Don't ye somehow get the notion that it's gonna be a long trip to New Mexico?"

This time Joe couldn't help laughing. He threw back his head and roared in laughter. He walked over to the stage and looked in at Harlon Claxton. He was still lying on the seat, his eyes closed but he was breathing much easier now. He must have heard Joe approaching. He opened his eyes and sat up.

"Is it time to go?" he asked. He opened the door and stepped outside. There was a little more color in his face now and he looked a lot better.

"The rest did you a lot of good," Joe observed nodding, smiling up at the tall emaciated man standing by the stage.

"Thanks," Harlon said, climbing up on the seat. He picked up his hat and put it on at a rakish angle. "I'm glad we stopped. I do feel better. Maybe the horses won't need to rest that soon any more."

"If they do," Joe said, a crooked grin pulling his mouth to one side, "don't worry about it. Just tell me when your horse," he paused and cleared his throat, "needs rest." He turned around and looked at Dorthea Claxton who was still sitting on the log. "Ma'am," he called out, jerking his head quickly, "we're ready to leave. The horses feel fine."

Mrs. Major Dorthea Claxton heaved herself up from the log and stomped toward the stage, aggravation all over her flushed face. She didn't say a word, just climbed into the stagecoach and slammed the door shut.

The two wagons and stage moved along at a steady pace until noon. They'd stopped several times to actually rest the horses but now was a time to really rest and eat.

It was a good thing the food end of the trip hadn't been left up to Joe. He hadn't thought it was his responsibility anyway and there was only a piece of jerky in his saddlebag. But he was used to being out by himself and living off the land. But Mrs. Major Dorthea Claxton seemed to have her fingers on all of the details.

"I assume that we're going to be here long enough for a good meal," she said haughtily, throwing a hot look at Joe.

"Yes, ma'am, you can assume that," Joe replied, swinging down and tying Sarge to a small scrub tree. "We could be here a couple of hours."

"Harlon," she called out as Claxton climbed slowly down from the stage, "do you feel like getting the food box from the back of the stage?"

"Sure," Harlon said quietly, walking toward the back of the stage in slow, dragging steps. Joe believed that Mrs. Major Dorthea Claxton would want Harlon to get out of his grave to do something for her.

"I'll help you," Joe offered, glancing in disgust from her to Harlon. The two men walked to the back of the stage and Joe got another surprise when Harlon lifted up the flap. As soon as the leather flap was raised Joe remembered what Dorthea Claxton had said about taking a bath at least every other day. He'd wondered how she'd do it. But as soon as he saw the white oval bath tub he knew how she did it. He looked up and was embarrassed to find Harlon Claxton watching him, a smug grin on his thin mouth.

"You didn't think she'd bathe in a water bucket, did you?" Claxton asked cryptically, the grin spreading all over his face.

"I had no idea what she was going to use," Joe answered, shaking his head, and gesturing with his hands, palms up.

"Well, I'm hungry," Harlon said, reaching in beside the tub for the wooden food box. "Bring that frying pan, coffee pot and bread pan." Joe picked up the requested utensils and followed him.

It wasn't long before Mrs. Major Dorthea Claxton had fried several potatoes, made coffee and cornbread. The four men ate like they'd never tasted anything so good before. Dorthea Claxton just picked at her food. After they'd all eaten and cleared the things up Joe tightened the cinch on Sarge and climbed up.

"I'm going to ride out for a while," he said, pulling his black hat down low on his forehead against the glare of the sun.

As soon as Joe rode away, leaving the four people watching his departure, he doubted the merit of his decision. An uneasy feeling pulled a tightness between his shoulders. He could swear that the short hairs on the back of his neck were standing out straight enough to hang a wash on. He'd had this feeling before and knew what it meant.

He was being watched. Actually from the time they'd left Fort Davis he had the feeling that someone was watching every move they'd made. He wondered if the eyes watching him now were the same ones who'd been watching him at the pond back at the fort.

But that wasn't what was really bothering him. He couldn't actually explain why he felt as he did. Maybe I'm just imagining things, Joe told himself, shaking his head in a quick motion to get rid of the feeling.

He had planned to ride at least three hours ahead of the wagons and stage and let them catch up with him. His main objective was to find a stream, pond or any kind of watering hole for the horses. There was enough water in the barrels for the humans and that included Mrs. Major Dorthea Claxton.

The desert stretched out for miles and miles like brown velvet in front of him, then a hill to the right broke the endlessness. Urging Sarge up the embankment he looked back eastward. The stagecoach and two canvas covered wagons looked like three child's toys as they moved along at a steady pace across the desert below. But even from his high vantage point he could still hear the harness chains jangling.

Joe pushed his black flat-crowned hat back and wiped his sweaty face with a salt-stained blue handkerchief. The dust from the two wagons and stage wasn't what had gotten Joe's attention. A second rise of dust to the right of the wagons and stage piqued his curiosity. From this distance it was difficult to see who or what was making the dust.

Reaching back in the saddlebags Joe took out a pair of binoculars and put them up to his eyes. He was surprised and a little worried when he focused on the two men riding at a slow but steady pace toward the slow-moving stage and wagons. Were they a threat or did they just happen to be coming this same way?

Adjusting the binoculars for a closer look, Joe got the answer to both of his questions. The two men, dressed in dark clothes, each carried a Winchester rifle and Colt .45. At the same time they turned their horses south. Joe knew that turn would put them in a position to come up behind the unsuspecting travelers.

Joe knew he'd better get back to his charges as soon as Sarge's long legs could carry him. Putting the binoculars back in the saddlebags he reined Sarge around, kneed him in the side and they started down the hill. Joe knew he could get back to the wagons and stage before the two men could reach it if he hurried.

Joe didn't know how good Bassett was with a gun but common sense told him that Boss Owens was along mostly for the ride and to drive the wagon. His gnarled hands would hardly be able to hold a gun.

Harlon Claxton probably wouldn't have the strength to thump a fly off his nose, let alone hold a gun or pull a trigger. Claxton didn't even wear a pistol. In fact his only weapon was a rifle in the scabbard by the seat on the stage.

True to his expectation, Joe pulled Sarge alongside Bassett's wagon shortly before the two men crested a hill behind them.

"What's the matter?" Bassett asked, a surprised frown on his face. He must have suspected from Joe's agitated expression that something was wrong. "I thought you were going to ride ahead for a while."

"We're going to have company in a few minutes," Joe answered, looking up at Bassett, shading his eyes from the sun with his hand.

"How do you know?" Bassett asked, standing up and looking back over his shoulder. "How do you know? Who? How many?"

"I was up on that ridge," Joe answered, pointing to where he'd just come from, "and I saw two men fall right into our tracks. Maybe they just started following us for the protection. I don't think they could know about those guns."

"Do you think we should stop?" Bassett asked, loosening the Remington .44 in the well-worn holster.

"Well, I . . ." Joe started to reply but was interrupted by a sound that was beginning to irritate him.

"Yoo hoo, Mr. Howard," Dorthea Claxton called, sticking her head out the stage door. "I thought you were going to ride ahead and find water for the horses. Why are you back so soon? Did you find water in such a short time?"

"I might as well ride back and tell her," Joe said, shaking his head wearily, "before she has a fit."

"Good luck," Bassett said, laughing. He nodded and sat back down on the seat.

Joe could see the dust cloud better now and knew it wouldn't take long for the riders to reach them. He'd probably have just enough time to explain things to Mrs. Major Dorthea Claxton, who was still leaning out the door, while the stage moved along.

"Two men are coming up behind us," Joe said, pulling Sarge closer to the stage. "They're both armed, but any man with any sense at all would be, out here in this country."

"Do you think they're following us?" she asked, pushing her windblown hair out of her face, "or do they just want our company?"

"I don't know," Joe said resolutely, loosening the pistol in the holster, "but we'll soon find out. Don't say anything about those guns," he cautioned. He was surprised and a little disappointed when she didn't argue with him.

Joe rode back to Boss Owens's wagon just as the two riders came up.

The two men, both older than Joe and Bassett but younger than Owens, were well dressed or would have been, if they weren't covered with dust, in dark coats, pants, white shirts and black plantation type beaver hats.

"Where are you folks going?" one of the men asked, riding up by Joe and Owens.

"To Las Cruces," Joe answered truthfully but still feeling that something wasn't quite right here. But then maybe he was just being overly suspicious because of the guns. To him everyone and everything was going to be a threat until the guns were at the fort and he wasn't responsible for them any longer. "How about you two? Where are you going?"

Joe watched and was bothered when the two men glanced slyly at the wagon and then back at each other. An eternity under the hot sun seemed to pass before the men answered.

"Oh, we're going to El Paso," the older looking of the two said, folding his black gloved hands over the saddle horn. "I'm Sid Daniels and this is Hugh Quintin."

Joe got another funny feeling that ran all the way down to his toes when the two men exchanged a quick look.

"How did you happen to see us?" Joe asked, resting his right hand on his thigh only inches from the Colt .45. He knew instantly that whatever their answer was going to be, he wasn't apt to believe it. The mountainous wasteland stretched mile after endless mile and a man could ride for hours if not days and not see another living human. Now from out of nowhere came these two men and almost crawled into Joe's pocket.

"Well, to tell you the truth," Quintin said, pushing his hat back on his head, "we stopped by Fort Davis to see if any wagon trains or patrols were heading toward El Paso. With all of the Indian unrest going on we thought it would be safer along with someone else."

If it had been at any other time and if the cargo was different Joe would have welcomed and even invited the men to ride along with them. The two extra guns would have been useful.

But now he wasn't so sure. Something about the way the men were acting caused Joe to wish that he was back at the fort. The fort brought Colonel Eric McRaney to mind. He didn't believe for a second that the colonel would tell Quintin and Daniels about them. They had to have been following them.

"Well, how about it?" Quintin asked, a hopeful look in his brown eyes. He pushed his black hat back on his head. "Can we ride along with you?"

Joe didn't want the sole responsibility of asking the men along and end up being blamed if something happened to them later on

"Hey, Bassett," Joe called out, cupping his hand around his mouth. Bassett pulled the wagon to a stop and stood up. "Get down and come back here."

Bassett wrapped the reins around the brake stick and jumped down. Spitting a stream of tobacco juice, he wiped his mouth on the back of his hand and in long strides walked back to the stagecoach which was between the two wagons. In the interim Boss Owens had left his wagon and the five men met at the stage.

"What's the matter?" Dorthea Claxton asked, opening the stage door.

"These two men," Joe began, jabbing his thumb toward the men, "want to ride along with us as far as El Paso. We could use the extra guns if we run into trouble."

Something in the back of his mind told him there would be trouble, but these men wouldn't protect them from it.

"What kind of trouble?" the always inquisitive woman asked nervously, her green eyes darting from Joe to the two men who were staring at Joe.

"Are ye fergettin' 'bout all them Injuns?" Boss Owens asked, a tight smile on his whiskered face. He turned away from her, then cut his narrowed eyes back to her. She glanced at Owens and pressed her lips into a thin line.

"No," she replied sarcastically. "I haven't forgotten about the Indians." She swallowed hard and took a deep breath. "But I'm sure that Mr. Howard wasn't talking about Indians." Turning toward Joe, she smiled slightly. "Were you, Mr. Howard?"

Joe shook his head in acquiescence. It's a good thing that God didn't have Dorthea Claxton around when he was creating the world, Joe thought. He would have had to rest on the sixth day!

"Ma'am," Joe began, pushing his hat back and taking a deep breath, "I meant trouble in general. Not the Indians in particular. I just thought we should take a vote on whether they ride along with us. It's not up to me."

Joe was surprised when the four people nodded in agreement all at once that Quintin and Daniels could join them. He was disappointed that Mrs. Claxton agreed so fast. She should have been more concerned about the guns. Somehow Joe just didn't believe that it was for protection that Quintin and Daniels appeared when they did. An idea popped into his head.

"In case we do run into any trouble," Joe began, a calculating tone in his voice, "I think it's only fair that you two know what's in those two wagons." He paused for a second, waiting for their reaction. When there was none, he continued: "There are six Gatling guns in those two wagons. We're taking them to the fort in Las Cruces. Mrs. Claxton's husband is the major there."

Quintin and Daniels exchanged quick glances then looked back at Joe. Something was definitely wrong here. He expected a more drastic reaction from the two men. He remembered how surprised he was when he saw the Gatling guns. He couldn't believe it! These two men were acting like they'd just been told that there were six bales of cotton in the wagons. Joe looked up at Harlon Claxton. He just shrugged his shoulders.

"You could be right then," Quintin said, nodding and pulling his mouth to one side. "Two extra guns could be a big help if you needed them."

When no surprise crossed the men's faces, Joe knew exactly where one kind of trouble would come from. He hoped that none of them would regret their decision in letting the strangers ride along with them.

"Okay," Joe said resolutely, pulling his hat down low on his forehead, "let's move out."

Knowing that Quintin and Daniels would try to take the guns before they reached the fort at Las Cruces, Joe raced his thoughts to come up with a believable way to keep the men as far away from the guns as possible. Then as if guided by divine intervention, the plan popped into his mind.

It had been previously planned to put the stagecoach in between the two wagons to protect Mrs. Major Dorthea Claxton. But now he could put the stage in front of Bassett's wagon and use the two men as outriders for it. That way Quintin and Daniels couldn't take them by surprise from behind.

"Harlon," Joe called out, more than a little pleased with himself at the idea, "pull the stage in front of Bassett's wagon. Quintin, you and Daniels couldn't have come along at a better time."

Joe wasn't disappointed this time when the two men exchanged surprised looks. He knew beyond a shadow of a doubt that he'd foiled their plan, for a little while at least, to take the guns.

Before Claxton pulled the stage out of line, Joe rode close to the door. "Ma'am," he said in a low voice so it wouldn't carry to the two disgruntled looking men. "I hope you have a gun with you and that you know how to use it. Don't ask questions," he hurried on when she took a deep breath, arched her brows and opened her mouth to say something, or ask something. "If one of those two men should come toward the stage in any way that scares you, shoot him. I think they're after the guns."

Before she could get her mouth going, Joe straightened up and moved away so Harlon could pull the stage up front. As the stage moved between Joe and the men, Joe pulled up by Bassett's wagon.

"How good are you with that gun you're wearing?" Joe asked, squinting up at the man holding the reins loosely in his hands.

"Well, I can't take the wings off a fly," the big man said, and grinned, "but I can take the rattles off a snake at fifty yards." He turned his head and sent a stream of tobacco juice the opposite way. Turning back he frowned when he noticed the serious expression on Joe's face. "Why?" he asked, staring down at the younger man. "What's wrong?"

"Quintin and Daniels just didn't want to come along with us for the protection we offer," Joe answered, narrowing his eyes and catching his bottom lip between his teeth. "If they hadn't known those guns were in the wagons, they'd have shown a lot more surprise than they did. They hardly batted an eyelash. I'm not sure when it will happen. But some time before we reach Las Cruces those two men are going to try and take the guns. I want you to keep a close watch on them. If either one of them does anything threatening toward Mrs. Claxton or Harlon, shoot them."

The day actually dragged by because nothing out of the ordinary happened. The only unusual thing, if it could actually be called that, was the castigating looks Joe got from the two men riding up front. He had dropped back by Bassett's wagon and knew exactly what was going through their minds. Joe knew though that he'd only delayed their plans.

What would he do if they made their move at night? How much help would Boss Owens and Harlon Claxton be? Boss Owens had been a soldier for a long time and had probably been in similar situations before and if age hadn't been against him, he could have probably held his own against anything. But years had stooped his once broad shoulders and put knots in the joints of his long fingers.

Joe knew that Owens had probably once been keen sighted but the white around his blue eyes had turned gray a long time ago. Boss Owens would undoubtedly do his best but would that best be good enough?

Harlon Claxton's poor health wouldn't allow him to contribute much to their defense, common sense told Joe. But Joe knew that he would do the best he could.

Something told Joe that W. C. Bassett was probably being modest in his ability with a gun. He was still young enough to be good enough with it and Joe felt a little better knowing that there were in essence two against two.

Since the two men had joined them so late in the day Joe decided not to ride ahead and look for as large a watering place as he would have done if they hadn't been there.

The sun was easing slowly down in the blue sky and losing some of its intensity. It still flamed the sky and pushed shadows eastward. A breeze as gentle as a woman's breath began blowing out of Mexico and across the mountains. Birds flitted through the few trees and their songs filled the air.

The travelers would have kept going until nearly dark but when they crested a hill and saw a small stream meandering south, Joe decided not to press their luck. Around the stream were several large oak and mesquite trees. There was an abundance of grass for the horses and wood for a fire. And Mrs. Major Dorthea Claxton could have an early bath if she wanted one. It would be an ideal place to spend the night.

"This is it," Joe called out, pulling Sarge to the left. "This is as far as we go today." He dismounted, unsaddled the seal-black horse and led him to the water. The stage and two wagons were pulled up under the trees. Dorthea Claxton and the four men went a few yards upstream from the horses for a drink and splashed water on their faces, necks and arms.

"Yoo hoo, Mr. Howard," Mrs. Major Dorthea Claxton chortled, wiping her face on the bonnet sash. Joe looked up to see her bounding toward him, swinging her arms like small pendulums as she walked.

If that Gatling gun was smaller, I swear I'd shove it down her neck, Joe thought, shaking his head mentally and starting to meet her. Why couldn't she just call him or wave a flag?

"Do you really think they'll try to get the guns tonight?" she asked in a strained voice, blinking her eyes rapidly.

"I don't know," Joe answered truthfully, as he took a closer look at her. Fear was alive in the woman's green eyes and her face was pale. "But if it was my plan, I'd get it done as soon as possible."

Joe couldn't help but feel sorry for the woman who heretofore had been mouthy, bossy and downright obnoxious when she, probably unconsciously, reached out and caught hold of his arm. He could feel her hand shaking.

"Don't worry about it," he said, forcing a smile. "You've got me, Boss Owens, Bassett, and Harlon. We'll keep the guns. How about some more of those fried potatoes. The others were good."

"Yes, that's a nice thought," she muttered, glancing nervously down at the ground, then up at him again. "I'll have Harlon get the things from the stage."

Joe turned around to get Bassett but stopped abruptly when he saw Quintin and Daniels still by the stream engaged in a highly animated conversation. It wasn't any of his business what they were talking about but in a way it was his business if it concerned the guns and he knew it did.

The two men must have felt Joe looking at them. They stopped talking and turned in his direction. In embarrassment they dropped their heads and led their horses to the trees.

Bassett came up behind Joe and startled him when he called his name. "Howard, from watching those two, it wouldn't surprise me if we weren't in for some trouble tonight."

"Why?" Joe asked, turning around to see Bassett looking at the two men through squinting eyes.

"I don't know," Bassett replied, shrugging his shoulders. "There's something about them that I didn't notice before."

"Yeah, I know," Joe answered, nodding and arching his brows. He wondered what had caused the change in Bassett. "Mrs. Major Dorthea Claxton is having second thoughts about agreeing to allow them to come along. She's really nervous."

Bassett and Joe shifted their gaze back to the stage where she and Harlon were standing at the boot. Harlon was bending over and holding on to the wheel. His face was almost purple and he appeared to be in deep pain.

"Something is terribly wrong with that man," Joe said sympathetically, starting toward the stage.

"You're right," Bassett agreed, falling into step beside Joe. "He hasn't been this sick before. He usually has a coughing spell every morning but recovers from it in a couple of hours."

When the two men reached the stage they were shocked at how ill Harlon Claxton really was. He was clearly trying to stifle a cough but didn't make it. A lung-ripping sound erupted from his throat and a thick yellow mucous spewed from his mouth. A shudder consumed his thin body and he collapsed against the wheel and his knees began to sag.

Joe and Bassett grabbed him and eased him around to the side of the stage and onto the seat inside. Gasping for breath, Claxton reached into his pocket and pulled out a white handkerchief. His thin and bony fingers shook as he wiped his mouth.

"Do you want some water?" Mrs. Dorthea Claxton asked in a soft voice that surprised Joe. She held a brown canteen in her hand. When Harlon nodded weakly, she handed the canteen to Joe and stepped back. Harlon raised up just enough for a couple of swallows then lay back against the seat and closed his eyes. He was completely exhausted.

"Can we do anything for you?" Joe asked, feeling

sorry for the wretched looking man, who slowly shook his head. "If you need anything, just call. Rest now." Claxton nodded, looked up at Joe and closed his eyes again. Joe shut the stage door.

Joe walked to the back of the stage. Mrs. Major Dorthea Claxton was standing with her back to him. Her entire body was shaking and he believed she was crying.

"Ma'am," he said softly, "can I do anything for you?" When she shook her head, he picked up the food box, Bassett got the utensil box and she followed them to a place under an oak tree and close to the stream.

Quintin and Daniels followed through on their promise to contribute food. Quintin opened the grub sack and took out a slab of meat. Daniels removed a sack of coffee from his saddle bag.

It wasn't long before the aroma of coffee, frying meat and potatoes filled the warm evening air and everybody thought they'd starve before they could put any food into their mouths.

"Do you think Harlon would want something to eat?" Joe asked, sitting down on the log by Mrs. Major Claxton.

"No," she answered in a soft voice, shaking her head slowly and expelling a deep breath. "He usually just sleeps after a . . . ah . . . . a thing like that."

Everyone was quiet for a while. The only significant sound was the scraping of knives and forks on metal plates.

"How long has he had these coughing attacks?" Joe asked, putting his plate down and sipping the strong black coffee.

"About a year," she answered, looking down at the ground. "But they seem to get worse every time he has one. I wanted him to stay in San Antonio or at least at Fort Davis. But he wants to make sure the guns get to the fort at Las Cruces."

For some reason Joe just couldn't believe the last part of what she'd said. If it had been true, she wouldn't have thrown such a fit when they had stopped earlier in the day for Harlon to rest.

The sun had begun dropping down behind the mountains and the night sounds began filling the air. A coyote's lonely and mournful cry wafted across the vastness.

"What in the world is that?" Mrs. Major Dorthea Claxton asked, jumping at the sudden sound.

"That's the cry of the ghosts," Joe answered, grinning at her in the dimness.

"What ghosts?" she snapped, leaning closer to see him in the shadows. "What are you talking about?"

"Oh, there's all kinds of ghosts out here in these mountains, ma'am," Boss Owens said, trying to hold a straight face.

"There aren't any ghosts out here and you know it," Mrs. Major Claxton argued. "You're just trying to scare me."

Joe peered closer at her. Mrs. Dorthea Claxton was really scared half to death. Her green eyes were wide and even in the waning light he could see how pale she was. The land, its surroundings and inhabitants and the presence of Quintin and Daniels had taken away some of her steam.

"It was only a coyote," Joe finally said contritely, standing up. "We've got a long way to go tomorrow so it would be a good idea if we all turned in." He chuckled as he looked down at her.

"I'll clean up the skillet and coffee pot," Owens said, gathering up the utensils and smiling down at the shocked woman. "Hope Mr. Claxton feels better in the morning."

Dorthea Claxton got up from the log and walked toward the stage. Her shoulders drooped and her steps weren't as springy as they'd been earlier.

"Boss, why don't you take the first watch?" Joe said, giving the older man a meaningful look. It was almost seven. Boss's watch would end at ten. Joe would take the next three hours and that would leave Bassett with the last three hours. Surely Quintin and Daniels wouldn't try something this soon. Joe and Bassett would still be pretty much awake while Boss was on guard and then they would be wide awake when their turn came.

Joe took his bedroll and put it at the front of the first wagon. Bassett, watching him, got the idea and put his bedroll at the end of the second wagon.

Joe watched Quintin and Daniels exchange knowing looks as they took their bedrolls and headed down toward the stream.

"We'll pull out at about six in the morning," Joe called out to the departing men. Without turning around they waved back at Joe.

Joe kicked his bedroll out and dropped down on it. He'd learned from past experience to keep his boots on. Three years ago he hadn't been so smart, had taken them off and the next morning had crammed his right foot down on a scorpion. His foot had swollen so big that he couldn't wear his boot for two days. Since then the only time he slept without his boots on was when he was inside.

Night settled over the land and as the darkness increased stars peeped out like diamonds. Joe stretched out and hoped he could go to sleep soon and sleep the night through. But that wasn't to be the case tonight. He dozed, slipping into and out of a light sleep. Crickets, owls and coyotes didn't do much to induce sleep either.

A nagging question had been trying to surface in Joe's mind all day and it finally made it. Why did Major Claxton want only six Gatling guns? He should have had at least two more. If he'd gotten those six without much trouble, why hadn't he gotten at least two more, two for each corner of the fort.

I'll ask Mrs. Major Dorthea Claxton about it in the morning, Joe decided, turning over on his side. The night passed uneventfully and Joe didn't wake up until Boss kicked him on the bottom of the foot when his three hours were up.

"Okay, boy," he said in a tired voice, "everythin's in place and nothin's going on. It's all yours."

Joe got stiffly to his feet, groaning as he moved. "What are our friends doing?" Joe asked, pulling his hat down. Bending over he pulled his bedroll together and stood up.

"Sleeping like two pups in the shade," Boss answered, taking a big yawn. "They didn't move a muscle all the time I was awake. I think we put a knot in their rope by puttin' the wagons like this and then sleepin' at the front and back."

Joe straightened up and laid the bedroll across the wagon tongue. "Well, we might have spoiled their plans for a while but they won't let it slide for long."

Joe picked up the saddle and bedroll and walked toward the horses munching on the grass by the stream. True to Boss's description, Quintin and Daniels were sleeping as though they didn't have a care or plan in the world.

Joe sat by the stream until his joints began to stiffen and got up and walked up and down by the river. The moon looked like a silver plate as it eased up over the mountains and was reflected in the water. His three hours took forever to end and his eyes were just about to close when Bassett came toward him.

There was no use to undo the bedroll again so Joe just sat down on the ground by the wagon, leaned back against the wheel and pulled his hat down over his eyes.

He awoke when the first rays of pink and orange began dividing the sky from the earth. Finally there was enough light for him to see to gather enough wood for a fire. The food box and grub sack had been left out and he got water from the stream for coffee. Bassett was washing his face and smiled when Joe put the coffee pot on the flames.

"Oh, my God, no!" Dorthea Claxton's shrill voice froze Joe where he stood and he stared at Bassett. The sound seemed to go on forever. For a second his body felt like it had ice in it instead of blood.

"What in the devil is she yelling about?" Joe mumbled, starting toward the stage, Bassett right on his heels.

Quintin and Daniels had been awakened by the scream and almost trampled Joe as they ran in the same direction.

Boss Owens was getting to his feet as the four other men reached the stage at the same time and stared in disbelief inside. Dorthea Claxton was holding Harlon tightly against her, his head pressed against her bosom. Something caught Joe's eye and he shifted his gaze to the quilt on the seat where Claxton had been sleeping. It was covered with blood just about where his face would have been.

Jerking open the door, Joe leaned inside and looked closer at the two people. Reality struck him just as Mrs. Claxton said: "He's dead. Harlon's dead." She raised her head. Tears were rolling down her pale face.

Joe motioned for Bassett to go around to the

opposite side of the stage. When he got around and opened the door he and Joe pulled Mrs. Claxton's arms away from Harlon and laid him back on the seat. Bassett got in, put his arms around Mrs. Claxton's shoulders and gently pushed her toward Joe and Owens. They helped her over to the log and eased her down on it.

Quintin and Daniels came hurrying toward them. "What's going on?" Quintin asked, a deep frown on his face.

"Harlon Claxton is dead," Joe said over his shoulder, walking back toward the stage "Would you get her some water?" He didn't wait to see what the man's reaction would be.

Joe walked up by Bassett and looked down at Harlon Claxton. The entire front of his shirt was covered with blood. Then Joe noticed that the blood had dried at the corner of his mouth. He'd probably been dead a good while.

"What do you think happened?" Bassett asked, shaking his head slowly and taking a deep breath.

"I would guess that he had a coughing attack," Joe answered, pushing his hat back. "I'm really surprised that he lasted this long."

Joe and Bassett stood there for a long time, or it seemed like a long time, looking down at the thin body on the seat and listening to the sobs of Dorthea Claxton. Joe would have almost bet money that this was one woman who he'd never see cry.

"This is going to change things," he said softly so only Bassett could hear.

"Why?" Bassett asked, jerking his head around and staring at Joe. "What are you talking about?"

"Well," Joe said, drawing his mouth into a thin line against his teeth, "either I or one of them," he nodded his head toward Quintin and Daniels, "will have to drive the stage."

"I could drive it," Bassett said, without thinking, hooking his thumbs over his belt.

"That would leave one of them to drive one of the gun wagons," Joe pointed out, cocking a brow and shaking his head. "That would be like putting a stray dog in charge of a soup bone."

Joe felt a light touch on his arm and turned around to see Dorthea Claxton standing behind him.

"We'll have to bury him out here," she said resolutely, swallowing hard and dabbing at her red eyes. "Then we must be on our way. We have a long way to go." She stopped talking until she could gain control of her quivering. chin. Finally she took a deep breath. "I'll drive the stage."

Joe and Bassett just looked at each other.

Chapter III

Six people stood with bowed heads around the long shallow grave. There wasn't enough time to dig one very deep and the small shovel wasn't very effective against the hard packed ground.

Mrs. Major Dorthea Claxton had asked Boss Owens, probably because he was the oldest of the group and maybe because he had lived longer and looked at life more reverently to say a few words and a prayer over her son.

"Lord," Boss intoned, gripping his cap in his hands behind his back, "ye've knowed this young feller a lot longer than most of us have. I guess ye didn't want him bein' sick no more and ye called his name. I hope ye have a good place fer him so he won't cough. Let his ma know ye're close to her. Amen."

Joe felt a lump in his throat as he glanced over at Dorothea Claxton standing at the head of the grave while Owens prayed. She had gotten inside the stage, pulled the flaps down over the doors and windows and changed into a black dress and bonnet. Now she gazed down tenderly at the blanket wrapped body of Harlon Claxton, a soft and gentle smile on her face. She blinked her eyes rapidly and Joe was troubled a little that there were no tears streaming down her cheeks. Was Mrs. Major Dorthea Claxton so callous and determined on getting the guns to Las Cruces that she had no feelings for the son she'd given birth to?

But he knew from past experiences that people had different ways of showing their grief.

After Boss finished the prayer, Dorthea Claxton bent over, picked up a hand full of white sand and sprinkled it on top of the body. Then she surprised Joe by kissing the tips of the fingers on her right hand and pointing them toward the body. Boss helped her to her feet, she turned and walked slowly back toward the stage. She got in, shut the door and pulled the flaps down over the windows.

The five men hurried and filled the grave and placed rocks on the top of it. That should discourage predators for a little while. Joe felt a little sad knowing that they would probably be the first and last people to see the grave or even know who was buried there.

After the horses were hitched to the stage and wagons, Joe was just about to knock on the stage door. It opened and Mrs. Dorthea Claxton stepped out wearing a light green dress and bonnet. With an agility and expertise that dismayed Joe, she climbed up on the seat and picked up the reins.

"I'll drive for a while, if you'd like," Joe offered, looking up at her. Her face was pale and lines were etched around her mouth and eyes. She looked a lot older than yesterday at the fort.

"No, I'll do it," she refused in a tired voice, shaking her head. "But I'd like for you to sit with me for a while, if you would. There are some things I'd like to tell you that I think you should know."

Joe couldn't begin to figure out what she was

talking about and his curiosity was pricked.

"Bassett, I'm going to ride up here for a while," he called out, stepping up on the wheel. "Keep following the stream. Remember what I told you. Keep your eyes peeled." Then an idea struck him. "Quintin, why don't you and Daniels ride a little way ahead and see if you can find a bigger water spot for the noon stop."

Once again the two men exchanged frowning looks and Joe knew that he'd probably upset some kind of plan they'd had. If he'd been the two men he would have taken the guns as soon as he could. But without any argument the two nodded and started west. "What did you want to tell me?" he asked Dorothea Claxton, turning around on the seat and leaning back.

"I noticed the way you were looking at me at the grave," she said, taking a deep breath and flicking the reins over the horses' backs, "and I could pretty much tell what you were thinking. I love my son as much as any mother could." Her chin began quivering and she pulled her mouth in tight against her teeth. It was a while before she could talk. "You're probably thinking that just because I didn't cry and carry on that I have no feelings for Harlon."

Joe was embarrassed that she'd read his thoughts so clearly. It was as though she'd looked inside his head and saw the words etched there. He made no attempt to argue with her.

"Harlon had been sick for a long time," she continued, after swallowing. "His father and I tried to get him to stay at a hospital in San Antonio. But he wouldn't do it. We should have been at Fort Davis two days ago but Harlon had a severe coughing attack the second day out of San Antonio. I've cried for him every night for the past year. I knew he couldn't get any better. I knew that he was going to die soon. He isn't in any pain now and he isn't tired. He's at rest. There's no need to cry any more." Her voice broke, tears rolled down her cheeks and quiet sobs shook her shoulders.

Joe wished the ground would open up and swallow him. He'd never felt so stupid in his whole life. He wanted to say something but realized that there was nothing he could say. He'd never been any good at expressing sympathy anyway and there was no need to try it now. He knew it surprised her because it did him when he reached over and patted her hand. She jerked her head up and around and a wan smile pulled at her mouth. They rode on in silence for a while. Joe was uncomfortable in the situation. Finally he cleared his throat.

"May I ask you something?" he said, leaning forward and bracing his elbows on his knees. "Why did the major buy only six Gatling guns? Surely if he knew about six there had to be others around?"

"I don't know," she finally answered, shaking her head and taking a deep breath. She wiped her face and blew her nose on a white handkerchief from her pocket. "He said he was in a hurry to get to Las Cruces and couldn't stay in San Antonio very long. Maybe those men had more guns for him. Why are you asking?"

Joe arched his brows and made a sucking sound with his mouth. "Well it just seemed strange to me that a fort would need more than six Gatling guns if they were going to be used at all for defense. There should be at least two on each side of the wall."

"Maybe he can tell you more about it when we get to the fort," she predicted, squinting her eyes as she looked toward the looming mountains in the west.

"If you'll stop the stage," Joe said, unable to think

of anything else to talk about, "I'll ride for a while. I want to see what Quintin and Daniels are up to. But," he said, smiling slightly at her, "if you want to talk about anything again, all you have to do is call me."

When she stopped the stage, Joe swung over on Sarge and kneed him in the side and started west at a steady gallop. He'd ridden several miles without any sign of Quintin and Daniels. He didn't think they'd go that far out and away from the guns. He thought they would have stayed together and would have been easy to find.

It suddenly dawned on him that something wasn't quite right with the elements. The birds were quiet and the sound he heard wasn't the wind blowing. A thin brown-gray haze seemed to be rolling slowly toward him. He squinted to see better. The haze could mean only one thing! He was about to ride into a howling sandstorm!

Pulling back hard on the reins, Joe stopped Sarge. He had to hurry and get back to the others and help them find some kind of shelter. Wheeling the stunned horse around Joe kneed him roughly in the side and reached the stage and wagons in half the time it had taken him to leave.

"There's a sandstorm heading this way," Joe yelled at Mrs. Major Dorothea Claxton, waving his arm frantically behind him. "We've got to find some place for cover."

Panic gripped him as he hurriedly glanced around. He'd never been caught out in a situation like this before. All of his bravado and know-how flew right out of his head. He'd never felt so helpless in his life. The surrounding area didn't offer anything.

Boss Owens had seen him hurrying back and pulled his wagon up by the stage. The oath that burst from Owens's mouth was enough to turn a mule skinner's ears blue. Dorthea Claxton turned a brilliant red. She sucked in a deep breath when her mouth flew open and her eyes almost popped out of her head.

"Pull the wagons and stage close together," Owens yelled, waving his arm in a wide circle. "Put the horses together. Joe, get the canvas off the wagons. We'll put them over the horses' heads. Then everybody get in the stage coach."

Joe would have thought of grouping the horses and getting into the stage but he wouldn't have thought there would be enough time to waste on the canvases. But with Owens yelling out what to do and how, Joe, Owens, and Bassett got everything done with only a few minutes to spare before the sand rolled in on them.

Mrs. Major Dorthea Claxton had jumped down from the stage, crawled inside and untied the window and door flaps and had them secured tightly against the wall.

By the time Owens, Bassett, and Joe climbed into the stage, the sand was engulfing everything. They could smell it in the air and feel it on their skin and taste it in their mouths. From his previous observation Joe knew that the stage had been custom made and a lot of care had gone into making it tight. But like little ants the sand found every minute opening and it wasn't very long until everything was gritty.

They didn't know how long they sat there in the hot confines of the stage. Bassett and Owens dozed, their hats pulled low over their eyes and bandanas up over their noses.

Mrs. Major Dorthea Claxton had put her feet up on the seat, bent her head and tucked her skirt under her shoes. She'd tied the bonnet close around her face and closed her eyes. She rested her head against her knees.

Joe, sitting on the seat with her, tried to sleep but too many things kept running through his mind. Where were Quintin and Daniels? Had they been caught out in the storm? Were they lucky enough to find shelter? Anything was possible and if the two were intent on their plan to get the guns, they'd take every precaution to follow through with the plan.

Time dragged by on leaded feet and it was late in the afternoon when Joe pulled the curtain a small crack away from the window and peeped out.

He couldn't believe what his burning eyes were seeing! But it couldn't have been a more welcome sight. The sun was shining brightly and definite shadows outlined everything.

"Everybody," he shouted, opening the door. "The sand's gone! The sun's out!" He jumped out and looked around. Sand was piled up against the wheels at least four inches deep. But a soft wind was now blowing across the desert and would soon take the loose sand with it.

Mrs. Dorthea Claxton opened the window flaps and began dusting the sand from the seats and floor. She stepped down on the ground and shook the dust from her clothes. Taking off her hat she slapped it down against her leg and shook her head when sand flew from it.

The three men hurried to take the canvases off the horses, unhitch them and led them down to the stream. After drinking their fill the horses were hobbled in the lush grass and the dusty and grimy people set about cleaning up.

Joe glanced over at Mrs. Major Dorthea Claxton. She wasn't as proud and haughty as she'd been yesterday. She looked as dirty and grimy as he felt.

He wanted to laugh. I'll bet she'd really like a bath right about now, he told himself with a malicious grin.

Walking to the back of the stage, Joe raised the sand-laden flap and took out the oval bath tub. Mrs. Dorthea Claxton heard the racket and hurried to the stage.

"What do you think you're doing?" she snapped, the old fire back in her voice and eyes. But he noticed a tiny gleam in her green eyes and a smile pulled at her mouth when he put the tub down on the ground.

"Well, ma'am," he replied, his hands on his hips, "you look as dirty as I feel and I know I'm going to have a bath in a few minutes. I think you'd like one, too. I just can't tolerate anyone riding around with me with that much sand on them. I hope you'll remember that."

Despite her austere bearing Mrs. Major Dorthea Claxton nodded and the smile widened on her face as she hurriedly opened a trunk and took out clean clothes, towels and a bar of soap. He filled the tub for her from one of the barrels and stood with his back to it as she bathed.

Bassett and Owens took off their dusty clothes and bathed in the stream. After they'd finished Joe took his clean clothes and walked a few yards upstream and took a bath almost as good as the one he'd had at Fort Davis a few days ago. When he got back to the wagons he was surprised to see Bassett and Owens taking all of the Gatling guns out of the boxes and wiping them down with rags. They had piled their dirty clothes by the stream and Mrs. Dorthea Claxton had rinsed them out.

"Mrs. Claxton thought it would be a good idea if we cleaned the sand out of the guns," Owens said to the bewildered expression on Joe's face when he returned from the stream. Owens pulled his mouth into a thin line and blinked his eyes a couple of times. He was squatting down on the ground, a long barrel across his knee.

"Mr. Howard," Mrs. Major Dorthea Claxton said, coming up behind Boss and squinting a frown down at him, "have you ever seen how a Gatling gun works?" She looked up at Joe, expectation arching her brows.

"No, I never have," Joe answered, shaking his head slowly. He hoped that if she was going to give a demonstration, she was more adept at it than his gut feeling told him she was. "I've heard about Gatling guns and what they can do. But this is as close as I've come to one."

Joe watched almost in awe, and he knew his eyes were wide as Boss Owens continued flapping the rag over the long round barrel with ten cylinders on it.

Apparently Bassett was used to the workings of the gun because he climbed up into the wagon, opened a box and took out a double handful of cartridges. Reaching down he took the cleaned barrel from Boss, mounted it on a tripod, attached the magazine and turned back to Joe.

"Watch those two cactus under that cottonwood tree," Bassett said, pointing toward a green clump of cactus with yellow flowers on the top. He dropped the cartridges into the magazine on top of the barrel and began turning the hand crank on the right side of the gun while holding on to the handle at the back of the barrel.

A deafening sound erupted and bullets began flying out at a speed that chilled Joe down to the marrow of his bones. He watched the top parts of the cactus almost disintegrate before his eyes. He'd never seen anything like this before and knew he was watching with his eyes bulging out. Joe turned slowly back and looked up at Bassett, who was watching him with an amused grin on his weathered face.

"You look kinda sick, boy," Owens said, standing up and moving over beside him. He slapped him on the shoulder.

"That's the scariest thing I've ever seen," Joe said solemnly, shaking his head and swallowing hard. "I'll bet the Indians would love to get their hands on something like that."

"Nope," Owens answered, shaking his head and arching his bushy brows, drawing his mouth down at the corners. "Not the Indians. It's too much trouble fer 'um to fool with. They like to use ambushes and a Gatling gun would be too long and heavy to carry into a close place."

There was certainty in the old man's words and he didn't seem to be bragging in his knowledge. He'd probably seen or at least heard enough in his years at the fort to pass away a lot of time in relating his adventures around a campfire or pot-bellied stove in the barracks.

"The Mexican army's the one who'd like to get their grubby mitts on guns like these," Owens went on, a disgruntled look narrowing his eyes.

"Why the Mexicans?" Joe asked, a frown pulling three lines between his brows. Were Quintin and Daniels planning to get the guns and sell them to Mexicans?

"Well, because," Owens began, a half irritated, half complacent smile on his face, "they . . ."

But he was interrupted by two fast running horses.

"Thank God we heard the noise," Quintin said, pulling his horse to a hunkering stop. He took off the new hat and slapped it against his leg, causing a small cloud of dust to fly. "Daniels and I got lost in all the sand. When it cleared away we couldn't tell which way to go. If we hadn't heard it we could still have been going around in circles." Daniels rode up by Quintin and the two men exchanged a smile.

Joe didn't believe a word Quintin had said. All they had to do was look at their shadows and go south until they found the stream, then either wait for them or go back east a little way or head west if they found any kind of tracks.

"We were quite a ways ahead," Daniels said, wiping a handkerchief across his face, "and I guess we got turned around. I didn't know a gun like that could make so much noise." A baby couldn't have looked any more innocent. Joe expected to see sugar dripping from the man's tongue at any second.

Daniels shook his head, stuck his finger in his right ear, wiggled it around and pulled it out.

"Mr. Howard," Mrs. Major Dorthea Claxton said, glancing quickly from Quintin to Daniels and back to Joe, "are we going any farther today or are we going to stop here for the night?"

Joe removed his hat, shading his eyes from the sun with it, and looked up at the clear blue sky. Only a few white clouds floated along. One passed over the sun that had slipped down farther than he was aware of. If his judgment was correct it was after two o'clock. They had lost three hours.

"Did you see any water as far as you went?" he asked Quintin and replacing his hat.

"Only a small pond," Quintin replied, shaking his head. "The stream runs out about a mile ahead." Joe noticed suddenly that Quintin and Bassett exchanged a look which Joe couldn't describe. Then it dawned on him that the tall man had exchanged the same kind of look with Quintin when the two men had returned a few minutes ago.

Joe hadn't noticed any familiarity between the three men when Quintin and Daniels had joined them yesterday. But then he hadn't been expecting any. Why had Bassett acted as surprised as Joe had at first seeing them? Maybe they had appeared sooner than Bassett had expected.

Maybe I'm just letting my imagination run wild, Joe told himself, shaking his head mentally.

"It wouldn't hurt if we pushed on a little farther," Joe said, looking around at Mrs. Major Claxton. "Do you still want to drive the stage or let one of us do it? I could tie Sarge to the back of the stage." Joe knew that she would refuse any help for obvious reasons but he wanted to volunteer before either Quintin or Daniels did.

"No, I'll do it," she replied quickly, tying the bonnet sash tighter under her chin. Common sense told her that it would have been either Quintin or Daniels to drive and she didn't trust either of them now. She'd missed the interchange of looks between Quintin and Daniels and Bassett.

After the men rehitched the horses to the wagons and stage the small caravan traveled on until there was only about an hour of daylight left. The sky was a watermelon color until the sun slid farther down in the blue sky, then turned lavender, then pink.

Joe had ridden ahead and found a level piece of ground under half a dozen oak trees. When the others caught up with him they all agreed that it would be a good place to spend the night. They hadn't ridden far enough to the water that Quintin and Daniels had mentioned but there was enough water in the barrels for that night.

After the horses were unhitched, watered, and hobbled, Owens and Bassett gathered wood and

Mrs. Major Dorthea Claxton made supper. The fried potatoes tasted good but somehow not as much as they did the first day out. They seemed to grind in the teeth. The coffee was still good though. Quintin and Daniels surprised everybody by volunteering to clean up the dishes. It really didn't take much since everything was sand cleaned first and then rinsed.

A strange feeling began to knot inside Joe's stomach. Premonition told him that if something was going to happen with the guns, the two men and possibly Bassett, it would be tonight. But since he had no way of knowing exactly when they would make their move, all Joe could do was go about his business.

He decided to take the second guard, letting Boss Owens have the first. He'd wake Bassett up around two in the morning. He took his bedroll, dropped it down on the ground at the back of the end wagon and kicked it out.

"Hey, Boss," Joe called out, sitting down on the bedroll and stretching his legs out, "wake me up around midnight. Don't let the wolves get you."

Owens, still sitting by the campfire with a cup of coffee in his hands, waved to Joe.

Mrs. Major Dorthea Claxton had gone to the stage as soon as supper was over and dropped the flaps on the windows and doors. Joe felt sorry for her. Her steps had been slow and her head bowed. She was probably thinking that this time yesterday Harlon had been alive.

Off in the distance, a wolf's mournful cry drifted across the wasteland. The moon was easing up over the mountains like a pale yellow ball and a gentle breeze with the scent of sage instead of sand in it would make sleeping easy. Whether it was the sound of the wind, or the physical and mental fatigue, it really didn't matter which, because Joe slept better in the next few hours than he had in a long time. He only awoke when Owens tapped him on the bottom of his foot.

"There ain't nothin' out there except more of nothin'," Owens said flatly, putting his hand over his mouth to stifle a yawn. "It's all yers, boy. Those two," and Joe didn't have to ask who, "are sound asleep."

Joe got to his feet, nodded, stretched the stiffness out and rolled up his blankets. He fastened his gunbelt around his waist and tied it to his leg. He thought about going on down to the trees where the horses were hobbled and tie the bedroll on his saddle but changed his mind and headed toward the wagons instead.

Joe was about two feet from the end of the rear wagon when he stepped on a twig, snapping it. In the night's cool stillness, the noise had the sound of a log breaking. He wasn't all that worried about the sound because he and maybe Boss, for a while at least, should have been the only ones awake.

He'd just rounded the corner of the wagon, lifted the end of the canvas and tossed the bedroll under it when he heard another noise behind him. It sounded like someone had also stepped on a log. Joe didn't have time or get the opportunity to see who or what made the noise.

The next thing Joe knew everything went black as a white shaft of pain exploded across the back of his head. He could feel his knees buckling under him and he knew he was going down but he never knew when he hit the ground.

Red and yellow and orange streaks of sunlight

were breaking over the eastern horizon when Joe finally forced his eyes open the next morning. He was stretched out on his stomach on the ground in the same place he'd been last night. From his low vantage point he could see ants going about their business as they hurried along on the ground. He turned his head slowly and wished instantly that he hadn't done it.

Another white shaft of pain shot through his head and little black dots floated before his eyes and he squinted them tightly shut. His stomach turned over and he wanted to vomit when he, with great effort raised his hand and touched the knot on the back of his head. It felt big enough to hang his hat on. He reached out and slowly pulled his hat toward him.

"Oh, my God," Joe groaned in a low, sick voice as he got to his hands and knees and finally managed to stand. The ground and sky wanted to switch places when he finally straightened up and looked around.

It took a few seconds, at least ten, for his befuddled brain to take in what was wrong with what he was seeing. Then like a bright bolt of lightning out of a dark cloud it dawned on him.

Both wagons, and that naturally meant the Gatling guns, and the stage, and that meant Mrs. Major Dorthea Claxton, were gone! When Joe's head and stomach finally decided to settle down into their proper places and stay there and his eyes could focus on one thing he looked around better.

A dark clump under one of the oak trees drew him slowly toward it. Chills ran up and down his back and once again he could feel the hairs on the back of his neck stand up. Joe couldn't believe what he saw! As he neared the tree he dropped his right hand down by his side. His hand automatically reached for the Colt .45 and for some unexplained reason he was surprised when he gripped the handle in his hand. Why hadn't Quintin, and Joe knew it had to be him because Daniels didn't seem to have enough sense to come in out of the rain, taken his gun?

W. C. Bassett, the very last person Joe expected to see in that condition, was lying on his back, his sightless blue eyes were staring up at the sky that was just turning a light blue. The tall, thin man was as dead as he'd ever be. Joe bent down for a closer look and felt under his throat although a wide red stain in the center of Bassett's gray shirt told Joe that he'd been on the receiving end of a bullet.

Joe stood up, looked around and tried to figure out what had happened. He heard the horses nicker and looked toward the stream. Two horses were tied where they'd been last night. It made sense that Sarge would be there. But who did the other one belong to? Of course, he told himself irritably: It belonged to Boss Owens. Remembering the old man, Joe looked around and when he didn't see him, reasoned that Owens had been taken to drive the stage.

In confusion Joe looked back down at the dead man on the ground. His death didn't make any sense at all. If Bassett, Quintin, and Daniels had been partners, why was Bassett killed? Had they gotten into an argument? What if they hadn't been partners after all? Had they jumped him as he was going on guard? No, that couldn't be, Joe finally told himself. He had been knocked out when he was going on guard. But then it finally dawned on him that he, Bassett, and Owens could have been ambushed at the same time.

Something else bothered Joe. Why hadn't they taken his gun? Maybe they thought the whack on his head would be enough to kill him. They just didn't know how hard my head is, Joe thought, a smirking grin on his face as he eased his hat down on his head.

Joe started toward the two horses when a low moaning sound pulled a gut-tightening knot in his stomach. He remembered telling Mrs. Major Dorthea Claxton about the cry of the ghosts and he wondered if maybe a ghost was after him now. It would be the only thing that hadn't happened to him.

He had only enough time to turn around toward the noise and jerk the pistol from the holster when Boss Owens stood up from behind a log. He carried his battered cap in one hand, was rubbing his forehead with the other and limping on his left leg.

"What in the devil happened?" Owens asked in a slurred slow voice, shaking his head carefully and squinting his eyes.

"I guess they finally did what we suspected they'd do," Joe answered, knowing how the old man felt. "I just didn't believe that they'd kill Bassett or take Mrs. Claxton with them."

"I thought they was all workin' together," Owens said frowning, putting his cap on carefully and shaking his head. He batted his eyes and looked around until he saw the dead man on the ground. He glanced back at Joe, a different kind of expression on his bearded face. "Ye mean they really took the old gal?" He pulled his mouth into a thin line and took a deep breath.

"Yeah," Joe answered, nodding his head and again instantly wished he hadn't done it. "We three," he motioned toward Bassett's lifeless body on the ground, "are, or were dispensable. But 'the old gal,' as you called her, will come in handy in a bargain."

Understanding narrowed Owens's eyes. "Wonder where they're takin' them guns?" he asked, gingerly touching the red mark on his forehead. "Wonder why they didn't take our guns?"

"I don't know," Joe answered, pulling his mouth in against his teeth, and arching his brows, "but we've got to get the Gatling guns and the old gal back."

Bassett's bedroll was still under the tree where he'd left it when he'd shaken the dust out. Picking up the blanket Joe and Owens went back to Bassett's body, wrapped it in the blanket and tied the ends around the feet and head with the leather straps.

The shovel was on the stage and there wasn't enough time to dig a grave if they were going to have any luck finding the guns and the old gal.

Many and various sized rocks covered the area around the trees and having no choice, Joe and Owens piled enough rocks on and around the body to protect it from any kind of predators.

This done, Owens saddled the horses and surprised Joe when he swung up on the saddle with the ease of a much younger man. He acted impatient while Joe checked his saddlebags. It took a little while for Joe to do it. Every time he moved his head, he felt like it was going to fall off his shoulders. When it was finally done, he swung up and he and Boss started riding west. That was the direction the tracks led and he couldn't be wrong.

Chapter IV

For a long time, in fact half of the morning the trail was easy for Joe and Boss Owens to follow. The deep ruts in the dry ground, especially those made by the heavy wagons with the Gatling guns in them, could have been seen in the dark.

The two horses were well rested. They should be, they hadn't been ridden in well over twelve hours. Joe and Owens let them run wide open for a short while and a lot of distance was covered in that short time. They finally pulled the horses down to an easy gallop. As they rode along the nagging question kept pulling at Joe's brain.

Why had Bassett been killed? What time had it happened? Which one of the two men had killed him? It was probably Quintin. Daniels looked like he didn't have enough guts to do something like kill someone.

Had Bassett tried to double cross Quintin and Daniels? Or had he tried to stop them and ended up getting a bullet for his trouble? Maybe his only concern had been trying to protect Mrs. Major Dorthea Claxton.

How long would Quintin and Daniels keep Mrs. Claxton alive? They already had the guns. Why would they take her along in the first place? The answer to that question popped into his mind as soon as the question left. They were going to use her as bargaining power. Would Quintin and Daniels try to sell the guns back to Claxton and if he didn't pay their price, would they actually do harm to Dorthea Claxton?

"Did you happen to hear Quintin and Daniels talking before all of this happened?" Joe asked Owens as they rode along. He reached up and patted his still throbbing head.

"Nah," Owens answered, shaking his head and pushing his blue cap back on his rumpled head. Joe wondered how long it had been since Owens had really washed his hair. "After I woke ye up, I started down to the horses to get my bedroll. That's when somebody whomped me on my noggin. The next danged thing I knew the sun was comin' up in my eyes." Owens wiped his hand across his face and Joe noticed the knotted fingers.

Joe didn't know how much help the old man would be in getting the guns and Mrs. Major Dorthea Claxton back but his plan, when he finally came up with one, would have to be foolproof.

The easy to follow trail soon ended around noon in a stretch of small loose rocks. Frowning over at Owens, Joe pulled Sarge to an abrupt stop. The trail had been leading northwest toward Las Cruces. But now the trail veered directly north. Self-preservation had taught Joe to never walk right into a situation when caution would prevail.

"Where do ye think they're headin'?" Boss asked, sending a stream of tobacco juice down to the dry ground.

"I don't know," Joe answered, drawing out the

words and shaking his head. "But unless they know a different way, they're not going to Las Cruces." He arched his brows and drew his mouth into a tight circle.

Joe and Boss followed the trail for an hour longer and were surprised when they rounded a hill and a short trail led to a burned out adobe mission. Joe wondered if the fire had been the work of Indians.

As they drew closer it was easy to see that it had probably been a beautiful place at one time. Maybe a year ago, Joe gave himself time to think. It had been made out of white adobe that was now scorched brown by the fire. The sagging roof had been made of red cobblestones. Some still hung on the edge of the roof and others were on the ground. A climbing red rose held on tenaciously to a black wrought iron railing, vying with sage brush and weeds for its place. It would take a lot of work for the place to ever look the way it should.

The two gun wagons were parked in front of the chapel and the stagecoach was a few yards ahead of the first wagon. Quintin and Daniels were sitting on the seats, looking as relaxed as if they were in someone's living room. Thick sage grass was hub high on both wagons and stage and that was going to be an aid in a plan that was beginning to form in Joe's mind.

"Wonder who they're meeting here?" Joe whispered to Boss, pulling his horse closer. The old man's eyes widened and he swallowed. He was probably beginning to regret coming along on this trip, Joe thought, looking back at the mission.

"I don't know," Owens answered, taking a deep breath. "But I thought they'd be a lot farther away by now."

At the odd tone in Owens's voice, Joe jerked his attention from the mission and looked around at him. His eyes were almost falling out of their sockets and it was easy to see that he was scared half to death. Apparently he'd never done anything like this before.

"You're not scared, are you, Boss?" Joe asked, holding his mouth straight with effort when he felt a smile pulling at it.

"Nah," Boss refuted in a gruff voice and shaking his head. "I jest didn't think they'd make contact with somebody this soon. This was planned a long time ago."

"Well, we're wasting time sitting here talking," Joe said. He pulled the Winchester from the scabbard and swung down. He watched Boss dismount slowly and knew that he was in no great hurry to get involved in something that could end up getting him killed.

"Let's leave the horses here," Joe said, tying Sarge's reins to a bush, "and go ahead on foot."

"Okay," Boss said pensively, giving Joe a push. "Ye go ahead and I'll be follerin' right in your footsteps."

Joe looked around. His shadow couldn't have been any closer than Boss. They turned and went around to the east side of the chapel to come up on the north side. They stepped as carefully as possible not to be heard and eased toward the front door. Now from this vantage point they could see the wagons and stagecoach clearly.

Joe felt sorry for Mrs. Major Dorthea Claxton. 'The old gal' as Boss had called her sat on the stage seat, her arms lying limply in her lap. She held the reins loosely in her black gloved hands. Mrs. Major Dorthea Claxton looked nothing like the snooty and obnoxious old crow he'd met day before yesterday. She looked a lot older and more tired than she had in the past two days.

Joe shifted his gaze over to Quintin who was leaning against the rear wagon wheel. He pushed his hat back on his head and there was an easy smile on his wide face. "They should be here soon," he called out in a voice loud enough for Daniels, and Joe and Boss to hear. "Chee Two Hats prides himself on being punctual."

Joe picked up on Quintin's sarcasm. Apparently Quintin and Daniels had a deal with somebody else. Had they planned on betraying and killing Bassett all of this time?

"I hope so," Daniels called back, a pinched expression on his weasel-like face. "He's already half an hour late and this waiting is getting on my nerves." He was squatting on the ground, pitching pebbles at a larger rock two feet away.

"Why?" Quintin asked, a grin sliding across his face. "You don't think that scout and old man are following us, do you? I tapped Howard hard enough on the head to put him out for a week. You slugged Owens hard enough to kill him."

So Quintin was the one he owed the favor, Joe thought maliciously, rubbing the back of his head.

"I still don't see why you had to kill Bassett," Daniels said in a remorseful voice.

"Will you stop your whining," Quintin reprimanded sternly, a dark frown on his face. "If I hadn't shot him, he'd have dropped you for sure. He had a bead right on your back. I hope you aren't getting too careless."

Joe didn't remember seeing any guns on Bassett. Quintin must have put them in the wagon.

"Wonder who 'they' are?" Joe asked over his

shoulder in a whisper. All he really had to do was mouth the words to Boss. The old man was right at his shoulder. The only way he could have been any closer to Joe was to have crawled inside the sweaty shirt with him.

"I don't know," Owens answered in a strained voice. "What are we going to do?"

Joe turned slightly to his right and looked at the old man standing behind him. He wanted to laugh at him but didn't. Fear was never a laughing matter. He remembered that Boss Owens hadn't been away from the fort in a long time. He could hardly call this mending a saddle.

"Well, what ever we're going to do," Joe finally answered, a definite look in his brown eyes, "can't be done from here. We've got to get as close to the stage as we can. I just thought of something."

Joe jumped up from his crouched position by the door, Owens still on his heels, and hurried back the way they'd come.

By the time they got back to the horses events had taken a different turn and a turn for the worse at that. Joe got one of the biggest surprises of his life and his blood ran cold, sending shivers up and down his back.

Three Indians, obviously Apaches from the way they were dressed, had ridden up from the west. Quintin and Daniels had left the wagons and walked over to the Indians.

The one in the front had to be Chee Two Hats. On his bushy black shoulder length hair were two dark blue Derby hats jammed together. The rest of his clothes were typical Apache. A bright purple shirt was sashed at the waist with a thin leather thong. Over the leather thong was a full cartridge belt and he carried a Henry .44 rifle. Light tan pants that fitted the Indian's muscular legs were stuffed inside leather moccasins that were laced up to the calf. Chee Two Hats sat a solid white mare like a bronze statue rather than a living person.

Black straight brows, over green eyes were almost lost in the low forehead. A chiseled nose divided his high cheekbones in a round face.

The other two Indians were similarly dressed with the exception of bright red and blue shirts respectively with matching headbands. The three Indians watched Quintin and Daniels with cold steady eyes.

Chee Two Hats looked past Quintin and Daniels and saw Mrs. Major Dorthea Claxton. "Why do you bring old white woman?" he asked in a deep loud voice. "She wasn't part of agreement."

Joe didn't know whether the Indian had meant for Dorthea Claxton to hear him or if he wanted to see how she'd react. But in any event his voice carried over to her. Joe knew that she wasn't about to let it slide by her.

"Oh, God," he prayed out loud, just loud enough for Boss Owens to hear, "don't let that woman open her mouth and say something that she, and maybe I'll, be sorry for." He closed his eyes, dropped his head and shook it in quick jerks.

But apparently Joe's prayer didn't have enough time to reach the Almighty's ears because he saw Mrs. Major Dorthea Claxton regain some of her former self-confidence as she drew in a deep breath, her shoulders straightened and her eyes began snapping. Flipping the bonnet ties back with one hand she glared over at the austere Indian.

"What do you mean 'old white woman'?" she shouted at him in a high pitched voice. "Apparently you don't know who I am," she chided through clenched teeth and tossed her head.

Oh, Lord, here it comes, Joe thought silently to himself, shaking his head miserably. Why does she have to be so danged proud of who she is? He knew perfectly well why Quintin and Daniels had brought her with them. Bargaining power. But he hadn't expected the Indians. Would her identity mean anything to this Indian and his friends?

"Ma'am, it doesn't make any difference who you are," Quintin put in, an evident warning in his voice, with a slight shake of his head.

"But . . ." she started to interrupt. Joe had to hand it to her. She had guts and white-knuckled nerve. Anyone else with an ounce of common sense would have caught on to the hint in the man's voice and kept their mouth shut. But not someone as conceited as Mrs. Major Dorthea Claxton! She was so proud of her position in life that she'd blab it to anyone.

A disgusted look narrowed Quintin's eyes as he looked up at the agitated woman on the stage seat.

"Ma'am," he said in a cold and level voice, "it really wouldn't matter to them if you were my mother. Now, shut up!"

Mrs. Major Dorthea Claxton sucked her breath in between her teeth and pulled her mouth into a tight line.

Something that Bassett had said yesterday suddenly popped into Joe's mind. When they had been cleaning the guns after the sandstorm and discussing who'd benefit the most from them besides the soldiers, he'd commented that the Indians wouldn't use them.

Now Quintin was dealing with the Indians. So maybe Bassett hadn't been partners with Quintin and Daniels after all. Maybe he had died trying to protect Mrs. Major Dorthea Claxton and the guns. That's why Quintin had shot him.

"When we get to Lac Cruces," Joe said under his breath to Owens who was right at his shoulder, "I'm going to beat the very life out of Major John Claxton. But right now we have to get the old gal and those guns back."

"How do ye aim to do it?" Boss asked, pushing his cap back and scratching his rumpled hair. He sucked a painful breath of air in through his teeth when he touched the lump on his head.

"I don't know," Joe answered dubiously, shaking his head. The words had no sooner left his mouth when the idea that had been in the back of his mind all along popped out. The grass was high enough and thick enough to hide a man if he squatted down.

Joe eased the Colt .45 out of the holster, spun the cylinder and checked the load. He knew the Winchester was full of shells. Squatting down he motioned for Owens to do the same. He holstered the pistol.

The old man frowned down at Joe until he realized what he had in mind, then he grinned. Owens envied Joe his youth as his aged bones rebelled against such unfamiliar movement. He just couldn't squat down and inch along like Joe was doing. The best he could manage was to bend his knees a little and lean over.

"Don't ye think ye'd better tell me what ye've got in mind, boy?" Boss suggested in a strained voice.

Joe turned around as best as he could in his cramped position and nodded. It was obvious that the old man couldn't read his thoughts.

"Let's try and ease down to the stage," Joe whispered over his shoulder. "The grass is high enough to hide us. If we can get her and the stage away that will be one less thing to worry about."

Boss Owens frowned at Joe. "Are ye crazy, boy?" he asked in disbelief. "As soon as we take off, they'll come after us. Especially Quintin and Daniels." He frowned deeper and shook his head slowly.

"How can they?" Joe asked contritely, a sly gleam in his eyes, "their horses are tied to the back of the wagons."

Boss pursed his mouth, thought for a second, then nodded.

For once since they'd started out on this sorry mission, fate smiled down on Joe and Boss. Quintin and Daniels were still standing by the Indians but had turned away from Dorthea Claxton. Quintin was saying something to Chee Two Hats but Joe couldn't hear what it was.

"Boss, could you get up there in a hurry and drive the first wagon?" Joe asked, gesturing to the one behind the stage.

A knowing smile slid across the old man's face and he nodded.

"I wonder if she's any good at driving the stage very fast?" Joe pondered, his eyes narrowing. "If she is, we can get both wagons and stage out of here."

Joe took a deep breath and started easing toward the stage. He'd have to hurry. His knees were beginning to cramp from crouching so long. He realized what pain Boss must be in.

His presence made the horses nervous and they began stomping around. Joe paused and peered through the tall grass toward the five men.

"What's wrong with those horses?" Joe heard Daniels ask. He saw Daniels move his hand toward his gun as he turned around.

"Oh, it's just probably a rattlesnake," Quintin answered dryly, and agitated look on his face. Both men turned back to the Indians.

Once again Joe started toward the stage. He eased up by the wheel, hoping and praying that Dorothea Claxton wouldn't scream when she heard him.

"Ma'am," he said in a soft whisper. "Don't look around. It's Joe. Keep watching those men. Can you drive the stage out of here? And I mean fast? Nod once for yes." He saw her stiffen in surprise at his voice and her head barely moved in the affirmative. "Boss Owens is going to drive the first wagon. I'm going to ease back and drive the second. Quintin and Daniels' horses are tied to the wagons. They can't come after us for a while. I don't know if the Indians will follow. Give me time to get back to the last wagon. When I yell take off like the devil was after you. In fact five devils are going to be after us. Do you have a gun?"

He remembered asking her that same question not so long ago. She'd said he'd find out in due time if she had one and if she knew how to use it.

"Yes, I have a gun," she answered in a shaky whisper, keeping her head turned away from him. "It might surprise you to learn that I know how to use it."

If Joe had had time he would have wondered why she hadn't used the gun before. Maybe she'd realized Quintin and Daniels wouldn't harm her and why. He did wonder though if Quintin and Daniels would try to sell the guns back to Claxton if the Indians didn't take them. Would they actually do harm to Dorthea?

Joe eased back the way he'd come. Boss was

standing by the front wheel of the first wagon, his left foot up on the hub. He was breathing hard and his weathered face was white. Joe pulled himself up over the edge of the wagon bed. The gun boxes had shifted over to the right side of the wagon and allowed him just enough room to slip down between the side of the wagon and box. Raising his head just a bit Joe could see the reins dangling over the seat. All he would have to do was reach out and grab them.

Glancing up and over the seat he couldn't believe his eyes and he'd remember forever what he saw.

Boss Owens had undoubtedly waited to see how and what Joe was going to do whatever he was going to do. He'd followed Joe's example and if Quintin and Daniels hadn't been so involved with the three Indians they could have seen his gnarled hand holding the reins. He raised his head just enough to motion to Joe that he was ready.

"If we don't hurry and get out of here soon," Joe muttered to himself, "that old man is going to be waving a flag. I guess it's now or never," Joe decided, taking a deep breath.

"Let's go!" he yelled as loud as he could. Slapping the reins over the horses' backs as hard as his crouched position behind the seat would allow, he rose up on his knees as the wagon lurched forward.

Boss Owens had more grit and stamina than Joe had given him credit for having. His wagon was moving as fast as Joe's. But Mrs. Major Dorthea Claxton was the biggest surprise of all. From where he was, Joe couldn't see her, but he could hear her yelling at the horses at the top of her lungs.

The stage wasn't as heavy as the two wagons and it didn't take too much time for it to be a safe distance ahead of the first wagon.

As fast as they could Joe and Boss climbed up on the seat. Almost at the same time shots rang out. One zinged over Joe's head, barely missing him. Switching the two reins from his right hand over with the two in his left, Joe pulled the Colt .45 from the holster. Turning slightly on the wooden seat he fired two quick shots mostly at the two men running and yelling at the wagons.

Joe was very surprised and greatly relieved to see the Indians still sitting on their horses where they'd been all this time. Joe looked back at Sarge and the horse that Owens had ridden. They were still standing where they'd been left.

"Sarge," he yelled to the horse, "come on, boy," The animals hadn't been tied all that securely and it took only a few tugs for the big horse to pull free. The other horse followed him and soon they were running beside the wagons.

Joe got another surprise when he turned back around on the seat. Mrs. Major Dorthea Claxton had turned around on the stage's high seat and was aiming a Colt .32 almost directly at him. Boss had pulled his wagon well to the left of the stage and was out of the way.

"Aim that thing at them, not at me!" Joe yelled at her, standing up and waving his arm frantically, indicating the men behind them. She moved her arm a few inches to the right and pulled the trigger again. The only thing the bullet would have come near hitting would have been a high flying bird.

Joe looked back over his shoulder. Quintin had stopped running but Daniels kept on coming. He fired another shot but this time Joe wasn't so lucky. The bullet caught him in the right thigh. The impact, feeling like a piece of hot coal, buckled his leg and he fell down on the seat.

Muttering an oath under his breath, Joe pulled himself up straight and looked down at his leg. Blood was already making a stain on his pants leg.

He glanced back over his shoulder and relief like he'd never known before made the ache a little less in his leg. Neither Quintin nor Daniels, nor the Indians were following them. He hadn't expected the two white men to be following them this far because their horses were tied behind the wagons. But he did expect to see the Indians following them because they were supposed to get the guns from Quintin and Daniels.

Suddenly Joe wondered what the Indians were going to give Quintin and Daniels for the guns. Would the trade have been made in money?

The horses had covered a lot of ground as the result of the sounds of the gunfire and the reins being lashed almost brutally over their backs. The pain in Joe's leg was so bad now that he gritted his teeth to keep from vomiting. He knew something had to be done but wanted to be far enough ahead of anyone who would be following them.

But now he felt safe enough to pull back on the reins and bring the horses to a stop. Standing up, Joe looked around and discovering that they were still out in the open, decided to go a little farther. By gritting his teeth hard he felt he could make it.

About seventy-five yards from where they'd stopped the ground sloped down into an arroyo. But that didn't suit Joe. If they were down in the arroyo and the Indians decided to help Quintin and Daniels and follow them, they could be picked off from the top. They had to go a little farther.

Joe endured the pain in his leg for a mile more but that was all. The entire right side of his pants was red with blood and his leg felt like it was on fire.

Topping a rise they saw a mesa with enough trees to offer some protection from the blazing sun and the other men if they were being followed.

Joe pulled the wagon to a stop but continued standing where he was. Boss Owens stopped his wagon, jumped down and hurried over to Joe. He climbed up in the wagon and caught Joe by the arm.

"Kin ye walk, boy?" he asked. Owens looked down at Joe's leg and shuddered when he saw the blood on his pants.

Joe nodded but decided it would be less painful to climb over the side of the wagon as it would be to walk to the end of the wagon and jump down. Feeling sick at his stomach, Joe leaned against Boss and eased over the side, sat down on the edge and eased his leg over the side.

Joe looked around when a motion to his right caught his attention. Mrs. Major Dorthea Claxton was scampering down from the stage seat with the agility of a woman half her age. The ribbons on her bonnet were flapping in the slight breeze and despite the gut-wrenching pain in his leg Joe felt a minute smile pulling at his mouth.

"Yoo hoo, Mr. Howard," she called out in her former tone, reaching the wagon and looking up at him. "Will they follow us here?" There was no fear in her question, just curiosity.

"If they do," Joe answered, bracing his weight on Owens's shoulder and swinging his left leg over the side of the wagon, "we can see them long before they get here."

Owens helped Joe down and hobble over to a tree. Joe sucked a painful breath in between his teeth as Owens helped him sit down on the ground.

"We'll have time to take care of your leg then," she said, turning and hurrying back to the stage. She untied the flap and took out a red wicker basket. Coming back to the two men she squatted down beside Joe and took out a pair of scissors. Reaching out, she started to take hold of his pants leg just below the bullet hole.

"Now wait just a minute," Joe protested, arching his brows and pushing her hand away. "I'm sure it's not as bad as it looks and Boss can do it." He could feel a blush creeping up his face but something in the back of his mind told him that he was wasting his time in arguing with her. There was a set and determined expression in her green eyes.

"Oh, pish tosh," she scolded, squinting at him and drawing her mouth to one side. "I've seen men's naked legs before. I had a son, you know."

Joe knew they were wasting time and decided to go ahead and suffer the indignity of letting a woman see his leg. If he argued with her, she would no doubt tie him to a tree and continue doing what she'd planned.

Seeing resignation on his face, Mrs. Major Dorthea Claxton cut the pants around and pulled the leg down over his boot. The blood hadn't had time to dry and she used a cloth from the sewing basket to wipe it away. Jumping up she ran back to the stage, got a pan and filled it with water. Carrying the pan in both hands she hurried as fast as she could back to Joe.

"Turn over on your stomach," she said, expectation on her flushed face. "I'll get the bullet out."

"Lady," Joe said wearily, wrinkling up his forehead, "it's because of you and those danged guns that this happened. I've had my head beat on, I've been shot at and now I've been hit. There's no way

I'm going to let you near my leg with those scissors. Let Boss do it."

Joe thought that his little speech would dissuade her. But his words fell on deaf ears. She pursed her mouth, narrowed her green eyes again and shook her head slowly.

"Mr. Owens's hands won't allow him to do something like this," she said, cocking her head to one side. "Maybe this will make you feel a little better," she went on shrewdly. Joe watched her intently. She reached back into the sewing basket and withdrew a bottle almost full of whiskey. From the golden color of the liquid Joe knew it was some of the best money could buy.

"If ye don't want it, I do," Owens said, licking his lips and rubbing his hands together. "That will ease the pain better than a sock in the jaw or a shot of mescal."

Joe couldn't stop the laugh that burst from his throat. It wasn't a bad idea. Reaching out, he took the bottle, unscrewed the top and took two healthy swallows. It burned a smooth path down his throat and on to his stomach.

"Two more swallows should do it," Owens encouraged, his mouth actually drooling for a drink. Joe didn't need much inducement to tilt the bottle up to his mouth again. This was beyond any comparison the best whiskey he'd ever tasted. Two more swallows like the first ones put him in a state of not caring if he stood naked before the entire world.

He felt Boss roll him over on his stomach and he winced only a little when Dorthea Claxton began probing with the scissors. He could feel the bullet scraping against the bone and he shivered. Twisting around he looked up at the woman he'd never have pictured in this situation. Beads of sweat stood out on her forehead and lined her upper lip.

"It won't be long now," she encouraged in a soft soothing voice. With one last probe she caught the bullet in the tips of the scissors and pressing her lips together, she pulled it out. Immediately bright red blood spurted out of the small hole. She pressed a piece of white cloth over the place and tied a long strip of cloth around his leg.

"Ye'll be as good as new when ye sober up," Boss predicted, helping Joe turn over and sit up.

"I'll need some pants," Joe said in a thick slurred voice. Mrs. Major Dorthea Claxton gathered up all of the utensils and started to struggle to her feet. Boss got up before she could, took her by the arm and helped her to her feet. Joe, in his drunken stupor, noticed a different expression on the old man's weathered face. A softness glowed in his blue eyes.

"The pants," Joe reminded in a level voice, reaching out and tugging at Owens's boot strap.

"Oh, yeah, sure," Owens muttered, jerking his attention from Mrs. Major Dorthea Claxton back to Joe. A pink hue was visible through his beard. Boss hurried over to Sarge, opened the saddlebags and took out a clean pair of pants, socks and shirt. "Are you sober enough to give yeself a bath?" he asked, grinning down at Joe.

"Yes, I can give myself a bath," Joe quipped and nodded.

When Joe nodded, Boss emptied out the bloody water, refilled the pan and set it down on the ground by him. There was a wide grin on Boss's face.

Joe waited until Boss and Dorthea Claxton walked a short distance away from him and removed what was left of his pants and shirt. He splashed the cool water over him and he had to admit he did feel a lot better, not to mention smell better.

"It wouldn't hurt you to have a bath either," Joe heard Dorthea Claxton suggest to Boss as she glanced up at him with narrowed eyes.

"Lady, we've been lucky so far," Boss contradicted, shaking his head slowly and hooking his thumb around his suspenders. But that same smile was on his face. "Them Indians could have given Quintin and Daniels their horses and they could be breathin' down our necks right now." To show her that the subject was closed Boss turned around and looked hard, shading his eyes with his hand, in the direction they'd just come from.

When the reality of Boss's revelation sank into Joe's inebriated brain he sat up straight on the ground, unmindful of the pain in his leg.

"Boss, help me up," He yelled out, holding up his arm, his voice less slurred. "We've got to do something in case we were followed."

Boss sauntered back to Joe, caught him by the arm and hauled him to his feet. Boss and Dorthea Claxton watched in awe as he limped over to Sarge, opened the saddlebag and took out a pair of binoculars.

Joe walked slowly over to the edge of the mesa, brought the binoculars up to his eyes and looked out over the sagebrush-dotted wasteland. A red-tailed hawk watched him from a tree. His blood ran cold at not what he expected to see but at what he really saw.

The three Indians with Chee Two Hats sitting tall and proud on the brilliantly white horse with a black blanket and rope halter were riding at a slow pace toward them. The other thing that popped Joe's eyes almost out of his head was the large white cloth tied to the barrel of the Henry rifle held high in Chee Two Hats's hand.

They were coming under the flag of truce!

"I don't believe it," Joe said, drawing out the words. "What in the devil are they doing?" He lowered his arm, shook his head as if clearing his thoughts and raised the binoculars again. The Indians were still coming at the same slow pace. Wonder why they weren't in a hurry? They had to know that he was hurt, Joe reasoned, and that they would have to stop sooner or later to do something for him.

"Where are Quintin and Daniels?" Boss asked, coming up by Joe and taking the binoculars from him.

"Well, since we have their horses," Joe said pragmatically, drawing his mouth into a thin line and bending his knee to take some of the pressure off his leg, "I guess they had to stay behind."

For some reason the words that Joe had just spoken sounded false in his ears. Something in the far recesses of his mind told him that Quintin and Daniels were as dead as the brown grass under his feet.

"What are we going to do?" Mrs. Major Dorthea Claxton asked flatly, bustling up by the two men and removing her hat. Her red hair had come unpinned and fell down in her face in untidy strands. She looked ready for anything.

Joe turned around and stared at her through narrowed eyes. A plan began taking shape in his mind and he hoped it would work as well in reality. He smiled slyly at her.

"Mr. Howard," she said, raising her thinly arched

brows, "I don't know what that smile means but I hope a good plan goes along with it."

"It will," Joe answered, nodding his head quickly. Hurrying as fast as his aching leg would allow back to the rear wagon, he gritted his teeth against the dull pain in his thigh, dropped the tail gate, climbed up into the wagon and using the butt of the Colt .45 loosened the top of the gun box.

"What do you think you're doing?" Dorthea Claxton asked, disbelief in her voice. She frowned up at him, her hands on her hips. If Joe had had more time he'd have drawn her a picture. But he didn't and was more than a little irked that she didn't have more perception.

"I'm going to give us an edge against those Indians," Joe replied, pushing the wooden lid back. Momentarily forgetting the pain in his leg, and it wasn't all that easy, Joe picked up the barrel and grabbed a tripod.

Boss Owens, becoming suddenly aware of Joe's intent, jumped up in the wagon, picked up a cartridge-filled magazine and clamped it on top of the barrel. Not knowing how much time was left and a lot had already passed since he'd first seen the Indians, Joe grabbed the crank and slid it into place.

When all of this was done, Joe and Boss looked at each other, smiled and expelled a satisfied breath. A sly grin spread across Boss's bearded face and a gleam pulled his eyes into narrow slits.

"Maybe we need one more edge," Boss suggested, pressing his mouth into a grin. He jumped down, if his unsteady movement could be called a jump and headed over to the other wagon.

"Mr. Howard," Mrs. Major Dorthea Claxton said when Joe started to get down from the wagon to go help Owens set up the other gun, "maybe it would be best if you stayed with this gun. I'll help Mr. Owens with the other one."

If Joe had suddenly been hit over the head with a rock he wouldn't have been any more surprised than he was by Dorthea Claxton's offer. Words failed him and he could only watch in stunned silence as she hurried over to the other wagon, the sashes on her bonnet flapping in the breeze as she swung her arm.

By the time she reached Owens's wagon, Boss had unlatched the tailgate. Owens's blue eyes almost popped out of their sockets when Mrs. Major Dorthea Claxton hiked her skirt well up over her knees, grabbed the side of the wagon and pulled herself up into the wagon. After Boss had opened the top gun box, Dorthea Claxton handed him the tripod and put the crank in place after he'd attached the magazine.

"If what I'm thinking should come true," Joe called across the short distance, "there could be more of them that we haven't seen or they could have split up. Why don't you turn your gun around and aim it behind us."

The words had no sooner left Joe's mouth when the white flag on the rifle barrel appeared over the rim of the mesa. That was the first thing Joe, Boss, and Dorthea Claxton saw. The first thing Chee Two Hats saw was Joe Howard crouching down behind a Gatling gun that was aimed directly at him. The other tow Indians soon rode up by him.

"Anything behind us?" Joe asked without taking his eyes off the approaching Indians.

"Nary a thing," Boss answered over his shoulder.

"What do you want?" Joe asked in a tight, but

level voice. He knew that the Indians spoke English because he'd heard them talking to Quintin at the mission earlier in the day.

"We come for guns," Chee Two Hats replied in a level tone. He looked straight at Joe, his black eyes never wavering.

The brown skinned man's nerve and audacity both amused and amazed Joe. Apparently the Indians thought that he and his two companions would just ride up, tell Joe that he wanted the guns because of an agreement he'd made with two other white men, and with no questions asked, Joe would smile and hand them over to him.

Peering closer at the Indian, Joe saw that he could have been called Chee Three Hats now. Quintin's new flat-crowned beaver hat had been smashed down on top of the other two the Indian was already wearing. Joe was certain now that Quintin and Daniels were dead.

"The guns aren't mine to give," Joe replied resolutely, arching his brows and shaking his head. "They belong to Mrs. Major Dorthea Claxton," Joe went on, but motioned with a quick jerk of his head toward the other wagon. "You'll have to do business with her."

The Indian's stolid brown face changed expression, if a minute twitch of the thin mouth could be called a change. Chee Two Hats's black eyes turned darker.

Joe heard the other two Indians say something to Chee Two Hats and laugh. The leader's face flattened before he whirled around on the white horse and glared at them. The smile which had softened his face died and quickly disappeared. Chee Two Hats turned slowly back to face Joe. The Indian's eyes were cold and he'd clenched his teeth together so hard that a knot stood out on both sides of his lean jaws.

"I do not do business with old white woman," the Indian said in a voice full of disgust and contempt. "I had agreement for guns with other white men. You come and take. Guns are mine. Not yours. Not woman's with busy mouth."

Suddenly a loud noise exploded behind Joe just as Boss Owens's voice called out: "No. Don't!"

Joe, with his hand still on the Gatling gun's handle had just enough time to turn around to see what had caused all of the commotion. Dorthea Claxton was standing like a dress-clad statue with a Smith and Wesson .32 short barreled pistol gripped in both hands. She pulled the trigger.

A low moaning sound pulled Joe's attention back around to the Indians. He wasn't ready for what he saw and wished to God that he wasn't seeing it now.

Chee Two Hats appeared to be falling from the white horse in slow motion. Blood was already appearing on the front of his purple shirt. His long brown fingers were groping at the front of his shirt as if he were trying to pull something out of his chest. As he toppled over the two blue Derbys along with the new hat that had belonged to Quintin hit the ground. The white horse stepped nervously to the left of the fallen Indian, her eyes wide in fright, her nostrils flared.

The other two Indians didn't waste any time jerking the Henry rifles up to their shoulders. Common sense told Joe that he couldn't outdraw them since they were already aiming the rifles at him and he had his hand on the Gatling gun crank.

Once again divine intervention took care of Joe

Howard. He was disgusted with himself for not thinking of the solution sooner! His hand was already on the crank! All he had to do was grab the handle on the back, aim the barrel and turn the crank.

Without wasting any more time, Joe moved back a step, bent over, and hoping he was doing the right thing, began turning the crank as fast as he could and still aim it.

A sound which he'd heard only once before echoed across the vastness and sent chills up and down his body. By the time he quit turning the crank and the sound stopped reverberating across the mountains and desert, the two Indians and two horses were lying dead on the ground. Everything had happened so fast that they hadn't had time to make a sound. Joe stared in disbelief and horror at the quick destruction on the ground.

The entire incident had taken less than five seconds! No wonder Major Claxton wanted these guns. With one Gatling gun at every corner of the fort he could hold off an attack from anything or anybody.

Joe felt as though he were standing outside himself and watching this unbelievable scenario happening to someone else. Taking a deep breath and shaking his head to clear his mind, Joe realized that he was definitely in the middle of it, that it was reality and not a nightmare. For a second he couldn't remember what had caused all of this. Then like a slap in the face, it hit him.

Mrs. Major Dorthea Claxton had gotten lucky with one shot and killed Chee Two Hats with that one shot!

"Why in the devil did you kill that Indian?" Joe asked incredulously in short breaths and frowning with two deep lines between his eyes.

"For one thing," she answered in a voice that seemed surprised that he would ask such a stupid question in the first place, and narrowing her eyes, "he insulted me twice. If you can remember he insulted me once by calling me an old white woman. He insulted me again by calling me an old white woman with a busy mouth!"

Joe could not believe this woman's vain reasoning. Her overbearing pride had caused her to kill a man who'd come to them under a truce flag! His intentions might have not been the most honorable but that would have had to be proved.

"That was hardly reason enough to kill him, for God's sake," Joe bellowed sternly through clenched teeth, glaring at the woman. Anger darkened his eyes.

"You're forgetting something," Mrs. Major Dorthea Claxton reminded snidely, tossing her head to get the loose hair out of her flushed face. "He also wanted the guns."

"Maybe we could have reasoned with him," Joe went on, exasperation shortening his words.

"And maybe the ground would have opened up and swallowed us," Boss Owens surprised them by interrupting. "We can't fix what's happened. We've got to bury them Injuns and get outa here."

Joe knew that Owens was right and nothing could be accomplished by arguing about it. He was made acutely aware of the pain in his leg when he started to climb down from the wagon. They could make better time if he helped Owens bury the three dead Indians.

This time they had the aid of the shovel and it didn't take long for three graves to mar the desert landscape that was perfect in its own way. The two dead horses were another matter though. They were too big to bury but would serve nature in their own way.

"What about that white horse?" Mrs. Major Dorthea Claxton asked shrewdly when they'd wrapped the Indians in their blankets, dug shallow graves and finally covered them with dirt and rocks. There was a gleam in her green eyes and a cunning smile on her thin lips.

"Mrs. Claxton," Boss Owens said, pushing his battered cap back on his head and grinning down at her, "with the right saddle ye'd look like a first class lady on that white nag."

Joe noticed the same grin on Owens's whiskered face as he tied Sarge's and Owens's horse's reins to the back of the wagon.

"You're right," Mrs. Major Dorthea Claxton agreed, tossing her head and climbing up on the stage. "Mr. Howard, can you catch her?"

Joe nodded and started toward the white horse. She began backing away but stopped when Joe began talking to her in a low voice. Taking hold of the rope he tied her along with the other two horses at the back of the wagon.

Joe wondered what else would happen to them before reaching Las Cruces as he climbed up on the wagon and flicked the reins over the horses' backs.

Chapter V

Joe kept standing up in the wagon and looking back over his shoulder as the wagons and stage moved along. He didn't know who or what he expected to see following them. He knew it wouldn't be Quintin and Daniels. They had been killed by the Indians. The Indians had been killed by him and Boss Owens and Mrs. Major Dorthea Claxton.

But he knew that someone with ulterior motives was following them, or watching them. The short hairs on the back of his neck were standing up straight again. Then a bone-chilling thought struck him. If it wasn't the Indians, who else could it be?

If he didn't have to drive one of the wagons Joe knew he could satisfy a part of his curiosity and scout out ahead the way he was supposed to do. But he also knew he wouldn't feel right leaving Boss Owens and Dorthea Claxton alone and defenseless.

Defenseless, ha, he scoffed to himself. Joe shook his head at his own lack of thought. Mrs. Major Dorthea Claxton was probably the least defenseless person who ever walked on this earth or drove a stagecoach. Maybe Robert E. Lee could have used her.

But he knew they'd lost a lot of time. Harlon Claxton had died and had to be buried. His death hadn't been caused by greed or selfishness. It could only be chalked up as the will of God. Nature had played a time-consuming trick on them by whipping up a roaring sandstorm. The rest was the exact opposite.

Quintin and Daniels had wanted and taken the guns at the cost of W.C. Bassett's life to benefit their own lowdown ugly way of life and line their pockets. They in turn had lost their lives because of the very guns they had taken from Mrs. Major Dorthea Claxton.

The Indians, for whatever their reasons, had wanted the guns. These same guns had cost the Indians their lives. Not to mention the two horses that had been killed.

It suddenly dawned on Joe who he expected to be following them. Those Indians hadn't been out on a fun ride and just happened to meet Quintin and Daniels. They were bound to be missed and someone would come looking for them.

These danged guns have become a curse, Joe told himself, a frown pulling his brows together and a knot bunching in his stomach. If he could get his hands on Colonel Eric McRaney right now he'd punch him in the jaw. The whole thing had seemed so simple at first. All he had to do was take Mrs. Dorthea Claxton and her son to the fort at Las Cruces, New Mexico. Now everything was becoming complicated.

Joe knew they had to make better time. But how? Once again divine intervention stepped in. They didn't need the stage. Maybe Mrs. Major

Dorthea Claxton did and maybe if things had been different the idea of getting rid of it wouldn't have occurred to him.

How much time do we have before the Indians come after us, Joe wondered, bringing the reins down hard on the horses' backs. That put more speed into them and Joe slowed them down when he saw a clump of oak trees.

"We'll stop here for a while," he said, pulling the horses to a stop. He jumped down and waited, leaning against the front wheel, for Dorthea Claxton to leave the stage. She walked over to him, flexing her fingers.

"Ma'am," he began, removing his hat and wiping the sweat band dry, "you're not going to like what I've got to say but it has to be done."

He watched her take a deep breath and narrow her eyes.

"Well," she prompted, plopping her hands on her ample hips, "get on with it. We don't have all day. Time is wasting."

Maybe this was going to be easier than he thought. "That's what I'm talking about," he ventured replacing his hat at a rakish angle. He felt more confident with her encouragement. Of course, she didn't know what he had in mind yet.

"We've got to make better time as you said," Joe began again, shifting his weight from his aching leg over to the other one. "I need to be able to ride a little way ahead. I can't do that and drive the wagon." He paused to see what her reaction would be. When she impatiently tapped her foot on the ground, he continued: "We've got to leave the stage."

Mrs. Major Dorthea Claxton's reaction couldn't have been any more dramatic if he'd said they were leaving her behind. "Leave the stage?" she screeched. "What about my things?" Her green eyes popped open wide in a glare at him. "I didn't come all this way to leave my clothes and personal things out here in the middle of nowhere! What's the matter with you?"

Her chest rose and her mouth pressed into a thin, tight line.

"We're not going to leave anything behind that you absolutely don't need, ma'am," Joe assured her, lowering his head and shaking it doggedly.

"Well, let's just see what I don't need," Dorthea Claxton said snidely. Grabbing him by the arm and breathing harshly through flared nostrils, she practically dragged him back to the stage. With a swiftness which belied her age she untied the flaps on the back of the stage and threw it back.

"I need all of these clothes," she said, pointing to the trunks and hat boxes. "And Harlon's things. I . . ." Her voice broke and her chin began quivering. She bowed her head and blinked her eyes rapidly.

Joe felt sorry for her but now wasn't the time or place for pity. "Mrs. Claxton," he began in a soft voice, reaching out and touching her lightly on the shoulder. "I know how much these things mean to you, especially Harlon's things. But, if as you said, getting these guns to the fort is uppermost in your mind, then we have to make some concessions. The four horses from the stage can add more speed to the wagons."

He saw the merit of his words soak into her self-esteem and she took a deep breath.

"I guess you're right," she relented, expelling a short breath and shaking her head in a jerk.

Joe couldn't stand the desolation of her demeanor. Mrs. Major Dorthea Claxton's pride and self-worth had taken her through a lot and had probably brought her this far.

"Pile as many hats as you can into one box," Joe yielded, shaking his head mentally. "We can transfer some of the guns to the other wagon and make room for the smallest trunk. Put as many dresses as you can into it. We'll need the food box."

A pleased smile brightened her face and she began to do what he suggested as Boss Owens unhitched the four horses and rehitched two to each wagon. Then he and Joe rearranged the guns to accommodate one hat box with ribbons hanging out and an overstuffed trunk.

Joe could never understand why women needed so much and could put so much into a small trunk when they had to. He shook his head slowly but adamantly when she looked longingly at the oval bath tub.

"Wait just a minute," she said slowly, walking up behind Joe and tapping him on the shoulder, as a thought struck her. She turned her head away and slid a look back at him. "If we don't need the stage," her eyes narrowed suspiciously, "and if you're going to be scouting ahead, that means I'm going to be driving a wagon. Right?" Her brows arched and she pulled her chin in.

"You're right," Joe conceded with a smirking grin. He tightened the canvas over the gun boxes, hat box and trunk. He was puzzled when he saw a look pass over her face that he didn't understand.

"Mrs. Claxton, what are you thinking?" he asked quickly, turning his head and looking at her sideways.

"Well," she said gravely, "if we can't take the stage with us, I'm not going to leave it for anyone else."

Before he knew what she was doing, Mrs. Major Dorthea Claxton reached into the food box and removed a small cloth pouch. she turned abruptly and hurried over to the stage. With her back to him and Boss, it was impossible for them to see what she was doing until they saw smoke beginning to billow out of the door.

"No, don't do that," Boss called out, hurrying toward her.

"I'm going to burn the stage," she said in an even voice. "Stand back or I swear I'll shoot you." Conviction was real in her eyes and she reached threateningly inside her blouse. So there was where she'd kept the short barreled .32.

It didn't take but a few seconds for fire to consume the interior of the stage and soon red tongues of flame were reaching the outside.

"Let's go," she said contritely, whirling around when she was satisfied that nothing could be done now to save the stage. She climbed up on the wagon, dropped down on the spring seat and gathered up the six reins. She waited, impatience on her face while Boss climbed up on the other wagon and for Joe to saddle and mount Sarge.

Joe made up his mind right then that when time allowed or they got to Las Cruces, he was going to sit down with this resourceful woman and have a long talk with her.

True to Joe's expectation the extra horses on the wagons added more speed and soon the smoldering ruins of the stage were lost behind hills, mountains, and desert.

The blazing sun had begun slipping low in the blue sky, stroking it with purple and gold. Suddenly Joe was acutely aware that they hadn't eaten since last night. He knew that Dorthea Claxton must be half starved. From watching her eat at other times he knew she had a healthy appetite. Rumbling sounds were emitting from his own stomach and he had to have something to eat. Wonder why she hadn't said something about it?

Fortified with the thought that nothing would happen to them the rest of the day, Joe pulled Sarge to a stop under a clump of cottonwood trees. Then they unhitched the horses from the wagons and let them graze.

Mrs. Dorthea Claxton was quiet and subdued while she went about making supper. Boss gathered firewood and Joe poured water from one of the barrels into the coffee pot. The tantalizing aroma of freshly brewed coffee drifted through the trees. The meat from Quintin's food sack sizzled in the much-used frying pan. Joe hurried and made flat bread.

When the meat and bread were done, Joe and Boss made sandwiches and wolfed them down with steaming hot cups of coffee. But Dorthea Claxton only nibbled at her bread and sipped her coffee. Since Joe and Boss hadn't eaten all day it didn't take long for all of the meat and bread to disappear.

Dorthea Claxton sat on a long piece of dead log, her elbows propped on her knees. She stared dejectedly down into the cup of coffee that was already cold.

"In a way I feel sorry for the old gal," Boss Owens said in a low voice, taking a sip of coffee. "It must have taken a lot for her to kill that redskin." The odd tone in Owens's voice drew Joe's head around and he smiled and frowned at the same time.

"Oh, I don't think it took too much," Joe argued objectively, shaking his head. He watched the old man from the corner of his eyes. "She said he insulted her and her pride couldn't take it."

"Don't ye think she only did early," Boss said, reaching over and refilling his tin cup with coffee, "what would have happened anyway?"

"What do you mean?" Joe asked, stretching his legs out in front of him and crossing his feet at the ankles.

"Well," Boss said pensively, taking another sip of fresh coffee, "it's simple. Them Injuns wanted the guns. Ye know as well as I do that there was no way on God's green earth that ye'd have let 'um have um."

Joe was silent for a long time, giving deep thought to what Boss had just said and realized that he was right. Mrs. Major Dorthea Claxton had only beaten him to what he would have done.

"I wish we had a better place to spend the night," Joe said, standing up and looking around. "There isn't much protection here," he went on, catching his under lip between his teeth. The area around them was flat with little or nothing to hide behind or under. Feeling confident that the three Indians wouldn't be missed this early an idea occurred to him. There were about two hours of daylight left and he'd have enough time for what he had in mind.

"Boss, I'm going to ride out a little way and see what I can find," he said, adjusting the Colt .45 down on his hip. "The two Gatling guns are still set up. If anything does happen, you and Mrs. Claxton should be able to take care of yourselves until I get back. Those guns make a lot of noise, you know."

Owens grinned and nodded. He got to his feet and threw the remaining coffee into the dying fire. Joe walked over to Sarge, tightened the cinch and swung up into the saddle.

"Yoo hoo, Mr. Howard," he heard Dorthea Claxton call out. He looked around to see her hurrying toward him. I wonder if she ever does anything in moderation, he asked himself, a small grin on his mouth.

"Just where do you think you're going?" she asked, her lips pressed into a thin line, her green eyes blazing. Bracing her hands on her hips, she looked up at Joe. He knew she'd stand right there until he answered her question.

"Well," he began, pulling his hat down low against the sun's bright rays, "I'm going to try to find a better place to spend the night. We are right out in the open and if we should be attacked by anyone there isn't much protection for us."

He felt sorry for her when her face turned pale and she swallowed hard.

"How long do you think you'll be gone?" she asked slowly, pulling the blue lace collar away from her throat.

"Not more than an hour," he answered. He realized that she was more scared now than she'd been when he told her that there were ghosts walking around in the mountains. "There's no need for you to worry," he said, trying to sound optimistic. "You and Boss know how to use those Gatling guns and you were pretty good with that .32 awhile ago."

Joe knew she wasn't reassured or comforted by anything he'd said. He also knew she didn't want him to leave when she took a deep breath and started to say something.

"Ma'am," he said, wrinkling up his forehead, "the longer I stay, the longer it will take me to get back. Just have everything hitched up so we won't waste any time when I do get back."

She expelled a deep breath, stepped back, he kneed Sarge in the side and took off at a fast gallop.

Joe guessed that he'd been riding about twenty minutes when he topped a small hill and started down. He couldn't have asked for anything better.

About a hundred yards before him was a ridge at least fifty feet high. A wide open-mouthed cave seemed to have been made especially for him. It had undoubtedly been there since creation but as far as he was concerned it had just been made. Kneeing Sarge harder in the side for more speed, the man and horse reached the cave in a few minutes.

Joe dismounted and tied the reins to a small rock outcropping. He stopped just inside the cave to give his eyes time to adjust to the dim light. It was hard to tell how far back into the hill the cave went without some light but Joe knew it would be a lot better than being out in the open for the night.

A noise in the dark recesses of the cave turned Joe's blood cold and he froze where he stood. It didn't take long for him to draw the pistol from the holster tied to his leg and thumb the hammer back.

Apparently someone or something had taken up residence in the cave and resented him being there. A snarling sound identified the inhabitant to being a member of the canine species. Joe could see better now and he eased a little farther inside the cave. Over in the corner, with three pups, was a large gray wolf. Her mouth was pulled back in a warning snarl which bared long white fangs.

Joe knew he had two choices: He could shoot the wolves or look somewhere else for a place to spend the night. He knew he couldn't kill the wolves. This had been their home first.

Joe started for the opening and once again divine intervention took the matter out of his hands. The wolf, her teeth still bared, rose to a crouch and growling low in her throat in a tone that the pups undoubtedly understood, led them in a mad dash past Joe, out the cave opening and down the ravine.

"Thank you, Lord," Joe said reverently, looking up at the sky as he mounted Sarge and took off at a fast gallop back the way he'd come no more than half an hour ago.

He wasn't disappointed when he got back to Mrs. Dorthea Claxton and Boss Owens. They must have been confident that he would find what he'd ridden out to find. Everything had been gathered up and put away. The only thing left to be done was to hitch the last wagon.

"Did you find a place so soon?" Dorthea Claxton asked, surprise all over her face when he pulled Sarge to a quick stop.

"Yeah," Joe answered, jumping down to help Boss hitch up the horses.

"Where?" she insisted, following right in his footsteps. "What kind of place? How big? How far?" One question followed the other so quickly that Joe didn't have time to answer the first.

"Ma'am, we could see the place a lot sooner if . . ." Joe wanted to say if she'd shut her mouth, but he only finished with "we hurry up and go."

Boss hurried over to her wagon and helped her

up on the seat.

Because of the heavy wagons it took longer to reach the cave than it took Joe to find it. He thought Mrs. Major Dorthea Claxton would be pleased that she wouldn't have to spend the night out in the open after so much had happened to them. But he was wrong in his thoughts.

As soon as she saw the opening in the hill she knew what it was and didn't waste any time in telling Joe how displeased she was. He was a few yards ahead of her wagon but it wouldn't have mattered if he'd been a mile. Joe would still have heard, "Yoo hoo, Mr. Howard."

Joe could tell from the irritation in her voice that he was in for a tongue lashing. He pulled Sarge to a stop and let her catch up with him. There was no need to ride back to her wagon.

"Is that where you expect us to spend the night?" she asked arching her brows accusingly, pulling the wagon to a stop by him. Joe knew from the angry look on her tight face that she was going to argue with him about it.

But he didn't have the time or inclination to argue with her about something that would be good for all three of them.

"Yes, ma'am," he replied shortly, giving her a no-nonsense look. She must have gotten the message because she only took a deep breath, swallowed hard and pressed her lips tightly together without saying anything.

Joe, remembering the wolf and her pups, and thinking that they might have come back, dismounted and went into the cave first. Surprisingly it was still empty and Mrs. Dorthea Claxton seemed to relax and accept the fact that this was where she'd be for a while, or at least until morning anyway.

Joe and Boss gathered up some wood for a fire and soon there was enough light to see a little way back into the cave. It was still empty.

"You know what would be really nice," Dorthea Claxton said, a little girl look on her face, easing up by Joe where he leaned against the cave opening.

"What would that be?" Joe asked, smiling down at her, having a feeling what she was thinking about.

"A bath," she answered wistfully, pulling her mouth in against her teeth and shaking her head slowly.

"Ma'am," he said, a devilish smile broadening across his face, "I don't see any reason why you can't have a bath."

Her face brightened when he turned and started toward the wagons. Joe took the tin pan she'd used when he'd been shot. It was deep enough to hold a lot of water and he filled it from one of the barrels. She hurried and got fresh clothes from the small trunk and followed him into the cave. Joe set the pan on the fire just long enough to warm the water then took it a little way back into the cave.

"Sounds like a blame fish flappin' 'round back there, don't it?" Boss asked, jerking his thumb backward. Once again Joe noticed a funny grin on Owens's face and he decided that now was a good time to say something to him about it.

"Boss, are you forgetting that Mrs. Major Dorthea Claxton is a married woman?" Joe asked bluntly. "We're taking two wagon loads of guns to her husband at a fort in New Mexico. Don't let yourself get carried away and don't get into something you can't handle."

A red blush crept up under Owens's beard and he ducked his head in embarrassment. "Naw, I wasn't forgettin'. I just ain't never met no woman like her before."

It wasn't long before the splashing stopped and soon Dorthea Claxton came up by them at the fire. She looked fresh and smelled like soap.

"Mr. Owens," she said, folding the white cuff of her clean gray dress back over the sleeve, "there's enough water in the barrel for you to have a bath, too. Mr. Howard had his bath earlier." From the way her nose curled up Joe knew it was more than a suggestion. Boss looked like he'd been hit in the face with a stick. His mouth gaped open and his eyes bulged out.

"A bath?" he repeated, arching his bushy brows. He glanced from Dorthea Claxton over to Joe and back to her. "You want me to take another bath. We just had one after the sandstorm."

She simply nodded up at him.

"Ma'am," he went on, a stubborn expression on his face, "if I take another bath, my hide will fall off my bones. I saved a little dirt and it's all that's holding me together."

Joe instantly threw back his head and roared in hearty laughter. Mrs. Major Dorthea Claxton's serious countenance crumpled and a real smile brightened her face. Her green eyes twinkled and a peal of laughter, which Joe had thought he'd never hear from her, burst from her lungs. She laughed so hard that tears glistened in her eyes and she slapped her hands together.

"A bath might impress her," Joe said cunningly, easing over and whispering in the old soldier's ear.

Boss froze where he stood, batted his eyes and couple of times and jerked a look around at Joe.

"Well," he drawled out, scuffing his foot in the loose sand, "I guess a little more water won't kill me."

If Joe hadn't been looking directly at the old man, he'd have sworn that he was watching a young boy with white whiskers on his face.

"I'll see what's in my bag," Boss said, starting to turn around to his saddlebag.

"Mr. Owens, wait," Dorthea Claxton said, holding up her hand to stop him. "I kept a few of Harlon's things." She shot a quick look at Joe. There wasn't an apology in her voice, just a statement. "You and he were about the same height. At one time he was as big as you are but . . ." Her voice trailed off and she hurried to the wagon. They watched her remove a pair of black pants and gray shirt. When she returned and handed the clothes to Boss he felt the pants were wool and the shirt was linen. He hadn't worn anything this fine in a long time.

"Thank ye, ma'am," Owens said in a soft gruff voice. Taking the clothes he turned and started toward the back of the cave.

"Mr. Owens," Dorthea Claxton called out, stopping him. "If you begin falling apart, I'll pick you up and put you back together again."

Boss drew in a deep breath, filled the pan with water, warmed it and took it to the back of the cave.

"Hey, Joe, kin I borry yer razor?" Owens called out, an excited sound in his voice.

"I don't believe this," Joe muttered to himself, opening the saddlebag and taking out the razor. Walking to the back of the cave, Joe handed the razor to Owens and stepped back out of the shadows. He couldn't help wondering how Owens would look clean-shaven. Going back to the cave opening he and Dorthea Claxton looked out over the country that had been just like this for centuries.

"Are you going back to Fort Davis?" Dorthea Claxton asked, taking a deep breath of the sage-scented air. "Or will you do something else after this is over?"

"Oh, I don't know," Joe answered, leaning against the opening, and bending his leg to take some of the pressure off his thigh. It still ached. "I'm getting a little tired of this kind of work. It's hard on the body." He grinned when she laughed at his jest. "I've thought a little about California. Boss is getting too old for it, too. He might want to tag along."

"San Francisco is nice," Dorthea Claxton said in a passive voice. "I was there once to visit my sister."

They stood there in comfortable silence until Boss Owens walked slowly up behind them, cleared his throat and then stepped out into the light where they could see him.

"Well, how do I look?" The voice belonged to Boss Owens. But that was the only thing that resembled the old soldier. The broad face, now shaven clean of the long-present gray beard was a pink color. The once yellow-tinged hair that hadn't felt a comb in a long time was now snow white, parted in the middle and waved back over the sides. Harlon Claxton's clothes fitted Owens almost as if they were his.

"Mr. Owens," Dorthea Claxton, cocking her head to one side and looking him up and down, shock all over her face, "you do look like a human being after all. For a while I thought you were a smelly old bear in a man's clothes."

Joe and Owens threw back their heads and ribald laughter echoed down the ravine. Night began settling over the land and the three people thought they'd have a quiet time with nothing to bother or worry them. But as the laughter died away, booming thunder, low at first, rumbled louder and felt like it shook the entire world. A bolt of lightning, like a jagged knife split the darkening sky. A low black cloud was moving up over the western horizon and they could smell rain.

Without wasting any more time because there wasn't much time to waste, Joe and Boss took the two assembled Gatling guns and positioned them on either side of the cave opening. Then they hurried to tighten the canvas tops over the wagons. Before they finished securing the second wagon huge rain drops began pelting down on them. Their clothes were soaking wet by the time they'd tied the last corner on the canvas.

The cave floor slanted down toward the opening but the rain was falling so hard that it collected in a small recess and soon spilled over a few feet. Dorthea Claxton gathered up her skirt and moved farther back out of the water.

There was nothing to do except sit, watch and listen to the falling rain. Once again lightning shot across the darkening sky, illuminating everything in front of the cave. Joe could hear the horses whinnying at the sound.

Joe didn't think there was any need for him or Boss to stand guard after they pulled one of the wagons across the opening. He brought in the saddlebags and bedrolls and spread out one for Mrs. Major Dorthea Claxton. In contrast to her character, she sat down on the bedroll, stretched out and went to sleep. Boss had taken his gear a little farther back in the cave and soon he was snoring.

Before Joe knew it he was awakened by a sniffing sound at the cave opening. He had slumped over and was lying almost on his right side. His arm felt numb. He had no idea how long he'd been sleeping. He listened as hard as he could without moving. He was suddenly aware that the sound was so easy to hear because the rain, wind, and thunder had stopped. The moon had come up and was throwing eerie shadows through the wagon wheels. It was then that Joe discovered where the sniffing sound was coming from.

Joe didn't think it was the Indians. They wouldn't have made that much noise. And if what he'd heard about Indians was true, they wouldn't attack at night anyway because they'd be afraid that if one of them were killed they wouldn't go to some special place.

Then he saw the wolf. She had come back with her pups. Joe grinned, picked up a small rock and tossed it at the wolf. "You can have it back in a few hours," he called out softly as she ran away with the pups right on her heels.

The few hours passed before Joe knew it and soon the sun was shining in his eyes. He got stiffly to his feet, walked over and tapped Owens on the shoulder, then called out to Mrs. Major Dorthea Claxton.

"Yoo hoo, Mrs. Major Dorthea Claxton," he said, friendly mocking in his voice, standing beside her. "It's time to rise and shine."

She opened her eyes, pushed back her red hair and glared up at him. "You've waited a long time to do that, haven't you?"

He laughed, nodded and walked toward the front of the cave where Boss was loading up the Gatling guns. There was enough light and it didn't take long to make breakfast and pack up.

"Yoo hoo, Mr. Howard," Dorthea Claxton called out, walking toward the wagon and tying the blue sash of a wide brimmed bonnet under her chin, a challenging smile twinkling in her green eyes. "Why don't you put a saddle on that white horse and see how she rides? I would but I don't have my saddle."

Joe could tell from the look in her eyes that she'd like nothing better than to ride the horse herself but there wasn't time for her to do it, especially if she was used to a sidesaddle.

"That's a good idea," he agreed, picking up his saddle and approaching the Indian horse. The animal's eyes widened at the strange scent and her nostrils flared wide. She'd been tied securely, as were the other horses, to a tree and couldn't go anywhere. It took only a few minutes for Joe to saddle her. When the horse finally calmed down, Joe swung up, let her dance around for a while then headed her out across the desert in front of the wagons. The white horse wasn't as easy riding as Sarge but that wouldn't take long to smooth out. Dorthea Claxton was going to have herself a good horse in a short time.

Time and miles passed. Joe kept looking back over his shoulder for some kind of sign that the Indians were following them. But there was nothing. He expected to see smoke signals from the hills and mountains or be attacked from the arroyos and ravines. But neither of those things happened.

Was it possible that the three Indians were renegades and working on their own? If that was the case, fine. There wouldn't be anything to worry about. But if not, it sure was taking someone a long time to miss them and come looking.

They stopped three times before noon to water and rest the horses. When the sun was directly overhead and blazing down they found a shady spot under some cottonwood trees. Mrs. Dorthea Claxton hurried and threw a meal of fried potatoes, bread and coffee together.

"When we get to the fort," she said, watching Boss Owens sand-clean the frying pan, "I'm going to eat nothing but vegetables for a week. I just might slip in a chocolate pie." She nodded her head slowly and smacked her lips.

"Sounds good," Joe agreed, transferring the saddle and blanket from the white horse on to Sarge. "She rides good, ma'am," Joe said to the questioning look in her eyes. "I just feel better with old Sarge under me. He and I have been together for a long time."

Joe was pleased and surprised at the good time they were making. If this kept up and all went well they could be at the fort in Las Cruces at least by tomorrow. His mind sighed a premature sigh of relief. He'd be finished with Mrs. Major Dorthea Claxton and the guns.

He wasn't sure if Boss Owens would go back to Fort Davis. Joe wasn't really sure what he wanted to do. He'd mentioned California to Dorthea Claxton last night. That sounded good at the time. He did know one thing for sure: He was tired of being shot at. A human being's body wasn't supposed to take that kind of punishment. His right leg still ached from the bullet he'd gotten yesterday. He knew there had to be something besides scouting he could do somewhere else.

Joe was so engrossed in his thoughts and plans that he didn't see the long dark object lying on the ground at a hundred yards beyond him. When it did dawn on him he pulled Sarge to a stop and, shading his eyes with his hand, squinted his eyes against the sun's glare. At first it appeared to be nothing more than a log. But there were no trees around that would make a log that big. Maybe it was a big rock or boulder. No, they wouldn't have been that flat on the ground. His curiosity got the better of him and he eased closer.

Joe could hear the wagons coming up behind him and he knew that if he didn't hurry up and find out what the thing was, Mrs. Dorthea Claxton would drive him crazy with questions.

Sarge rumbled low in his throat as Joe eased him closer to the object on the ground. Caution overpowered Joe's curiosity. Instead of jumping down to see what it was, he looked around to see if it was safe.

The only thing Joe could see was an eagle soaring effortlessly on the air currents in the blue sky and a sidewinder was hurrying across the ground to get out of the horse's way.

Satisfied that everything was safe, Joe dismounted, drew the Colt .45 from the holster and eased forward. He blinked his eyes several times and frowned at what he saw as his blood ran cold.

A Mexican, obviously from the wide-brimmed tan sombrero, brown leather leggings and two full cartridge belts crossed over his back was on his stomach with his hands under him. Just as Joe started to bend down and turn him over, a bell went off in the back of his head, telling him that he'd just made the biggest mistake of his life.

The man who'd been lying almost death-still

rolled over with a speed that brought an unbelieving gasp from Joe. There wasn't a mark or stain to indicate that he was injured in any way.

"Oh, my God," Joe moaned out loud slowly in a barely audible voice. From the sinister smile on the long, thin brown face, the gleam in the black eyes, but most of all the long barreled pistol held in the man's slender fingered hand and aimed directly at Joe's chest told him that he'd ridden into a trap! Joe knew instantly that there had to be a lot more bandits around. Were they the ones who'd been following them?

Joe was angry with himself and felt sick at his stomach for being so foolish and careless. Not only had he ridden into the trap, he was leading Mrs. Dorthea Claxton and Boss Claxton into that same trap!

Before Joe could think about moving or try to pull the trigger, and it would have been a stupid thought anyway, he heard horses' hoofs and voices coming up behind him. The ploy had worked well enough that the approaching riders didn't care how much noise they made.

"Señor," the man on the ground said with a wide smile that showed white teeth, "I think it would be a good idea for you to hand me your gun." Keeping an eye on Joe, the bandit eased almost nonchalantly to his feet as his companions came up behind Joe.

Joe knew he had no choice and using his left hand took the Colt .45 by the barrel and pitched it over to the brown skinned man still grinning sardonically at him.

Positive that he presented no threat now, Joe turned around slowly and looked at the advancing riders. Five more Mexicans similarly dressed as the one who'd been so convincingly dead on the ground only a few minutes ago pulled their horses to a stop. One Mexican was leading an extra horse.

"Bueno trabajo, Malito," the man riding in the front said in a satisfied tone of voice. Joe noticed that he was dressed differently from the other five. He wore a short leather jacket over a white shirt, black pants with conchos down the side and silver spurs with large rowels. He didn't wear the crossed cartridge belts but had a Winchester rifle in his brown hands.

The words which were foreign to Joe's ears were obviously a compliment from the wide smile on the man's broad face. Joe glanced back at the man still holding the pistol aimed at his back. Malito smiled and nodded his head slightly. *"Gracias,* Ortez."

"Habla espanol, señor?" Ortez asked, arching his black brows. Joe understood this and shook his head just as the two wagons appeared over the rise. Mrs. Dorthea Claxton's wagon was ahead and a little to the right of Owens's and it didn't take her long to assess the situation. Joe could almost hear the wheels spinning around inside her head. She'd pull the horses to a stop, crawl over the seat, grab the Gatling gun and do away with the bandits. or she'd try to take the .32 from her blouse.

But shock, age, odds and common sense told her to just sit still and keep her mouth shut. For once she listened. Owens was another matter. As soon as he saw the Mexicans, he lashed the reins down over the horses' backs and for a second they lurched ahead a few feet. Apparently one of the Mexicans had anticipated what Boss would do. He spurred his horse in the side, rode over to the wagon, caught hold of the reins and stopped the wagon.

"No, no, señor," the leader admonished, wagging

his finger back and forth, a patronizing smile sliding across his face.

"Mrs. Claxton," Joe said, desperation edging his voice, knowing she had the pistol on her, "Boss, don't do anything. They probably just want the guns."

Ortez threw back his black shaggy head and roared in laughter. "You are so right, *amigo*. Just the guns. Not the wagons. Or you. We could have used the stage. I do wish you had not burned it. If you will follow us." He indicated south with a jerk of his thumb over his shoulder, "we will unload the wagons and you can be on your way to Las Cruces."

The last part of what the Mexican said shook Joe right down to the soles of his well-worn boots and the hair stood out on the back of his neck. A knot pulled in his stomach.

He knew now that Ortez and his men had been the ones following them. But how did he and his men know they were going to Las Cruces? Swinging up on Sarge, Joe glanced over at Mrs. Dorthea Claxton and her face looked as surprised as he felt. She arched her brows and that widened her green eyes. True to her nature she started to say something but Joe shook his head. She pulled her lips between her teeth.

The trip to where the Mexicans wanted them didn't take any more than twenty minutes. Ortez held up his right hand for them to stop when they rounded a hill to come up in front of three adobe shacks. Smiling amicably but with a threat deep in his black eyes he motioned for the three people to dismount.

Joe expected to see more Mexicans come pouring out of the shacks but that didn't happen. He felt a little better. If a plan happened to come to mind he would only have the six men to contend with.

"Can I ask you a question?" Joe ventured, swinging down and holding the reins in his left hand. He touched the empty holster out of habit with his right hand and felt a little naked.

"Oh, sure," Ortez replied, a lilt in his voice. He dismounted in a fluid motion and turned to face Joe. He closed and opened his eyes slowly as if there was no hurry in the world. "What would you like to know?" He pushed the big hat back on his mop of black hair and hooked his thumb over the top of a silver studded gun belt.

"How did you know we were going to Las Cruces?" Joe watched the man. He knew he would tell him the truth. There would be no reason for him to lie.

"Well, it is like this," Ortez began, making a sucking sound when he pulled his mouth in against his teeth. "We have an arrangement with a gringo at the fort for half of the guns. But," he arched his black brows, smiled again and spread hands out before him, "why should we wait, go to the fort and settle for half of the guns when we can have all of them now?" Ortez clapped his hands together, a pleased grin shining in his black eyes.

"You have a point there," Joe agreed, nodding his head slowly. He wondered who the "gringo" was at the fort.

"Just who are you talking about?" Mrs. Major Dorthea Claxton asked, her chest rising and falling in quick breaths. She had been quiet as long as she could. Her self-esteem was back and she wasn't going to be treated like this. One of the Mexicans had helped her down and she was glaring at Ortez. "Do you know who I am?"

Here we go again, Joe thought to himself, taking a deep breath.

"Well, let me tell you just in case you don't know," she hurried on. "I'm Mrs. Major Edward Claxton. My husband is the commandant at the fort in Las Cruces. If you try and take these guns he will get a patrol and hunt you down. Then he will arrest whoever is selling you these guns."

Obviously the Mexicans were more tolerant of white women and their prattling tongues than the Indians were. Ortez stared passively at her and listened to her ramble on. When she'd finally hushed he made a pretense of a bow and tipped his head forward a little.

"Oh, sí, señora," Ortez said, straightening up and pulling the big hat low on his forehead. "We have known all along who you are. You had a son named Harlon. He died several days ago. I am very sorry." He smiled when she gasped and saw the surprised frown on Joe's face.

"How did you know about Harlon?" Mrs. Major Dorthea Claxton asked, taking an unconscious step toward the Mexican.

"I am not stupid, Señora Claxton," Ortez replied, holding up a warning hand. Joe, realizing what her folly could do, reached out and grabbed her by the arm and held her back. "There are ways to find out things," Ortez went on. "But mostly your husband told me about you and your son. The only thing he didn't tell me was that Harlon was dead. This he doesn't know yet."

Joe didn't want to believe the idea that was forming in the back of his mind. It just wouldn't make sense. But everything fell into place now. Ortez and his men were the ones who had been following them all of this time. He was, in one sense of the word, taking care of his guns.

"Why would the major tell ye all of this stuff?" Boss Owens asked, climbing down from his wagon. "Who do you have a deal with?"

Everybody seemed to have forgotten about the older man who was now standing by the wagon and turned at the sound of his gruff voice.

Once again Ortez hooked his thumbs over the top of his belt and he smiled.

"I have," he said, stressing the word, "a deal with Major Eduardo Claxton." His eyes narrowed as he turned slowly and faced Mrs. Dorthea Claxton. Her face turned white and her mouth flew open. But this time words failed her. She began sagging and probably for the first time in her entire life, Dorthea Claxton fainted. Joe caught her before she hit the ground and eased her up against the wagon wheel.

"Why would a major in the U. S. Army want to make a deal with you?" Joe asked, squatting beside the woman and looking up at Ortez.

"It is simple," Ortez answered, shrugging his shoulders and rubbing his thumb and fingers together. "*Dinero*. Money." Then he shook his head. "But enough talk for now. *Muchachos,* start unloading those guns."

Joe felt helpless watching the Mexicans untie the ropes and throw back the canvases from the gun boxes. Then his helpless feeling was overcome by anger when he thought about how close they were to the fort and ending up losing the guns after all. His anger intensified when he thought about Major Edward Claxton's deal with Ortez and his men for the guns. The guns he had already killed for! Guns that his wife had killed for! It ranked him to think that he'd come this far for nothing.

Ortez had said they could go after the guns were unloaded. What would he really have to gain by killing the three people if they didn't put up a fight? Reality should tell the bandit that as soon as they reached the fort and Claxton learned that the guns were gone, he'd send a patrol after him.

But if Ortez was over in Mexico the troops couldn't go after him in any official capacity. How was Claxton going to explain his part in a deal with Ortez to his wife? How much money was involved?

If Ortez took all of the guns as he was very obviously doing, what would Claxton's reaction be when his wife reached the fort without them? That would be something worth seeing!

A thought struck Joe. Had Claxton been doing business with Ortez before now? How much was Ortez paying him and in what?

If Joe could have gotten his hands on Major Edward Claxton right at that minute, he would have killed him with no questions asked! What kind of man would endanger the life of his wife and son, especially a son who was ill, for something like this?

But what if Ortez was lying? Joe knew that part of what the bandit had said was true. He knew that Harlon Claxton was dead.

Was Ortez lying about the guns? Was he lying about having a deal with Major Edward Claxton? It was hard to believe from looking at Mrs. Dorthea Claxton who was regaining consciousness on the ground, that she'd be married to a man like that without knowing it.

Joe helped Dorthea Claxton to her feet and immediately she started in on the unsuspecting Ortez.

"Are you sure you're talking about the right Major Edward Claxton?" she asked, desperation in her green eyes and voice. Joe thought he saw her chin quiver but wouldn't swear to it. "It could have been someone else passing himself off as Edward. My husband wouldn't do something like this. He's too honorable."

Joe did see her chin quiver this time and a tear rolled down her pale cheek. She'd put words to an idea that he hadn't thought of.

"Ah, Señora Claxton," Ortez said in a soft and pitying voice and shaking his head slowly. "I am sure we are talking about the same man. About as tall as you. Fat around . . ." Ortez patted his own middle for reference. "Gray-black hair and . . ." He stopped his description when Dorthea Claxton clapped her hands over her eyes and began crying hysterically. Boss Owens, concern all over his wrinkled face, hurried over to her, put his arm protectively around her shoulders and was surprised when she fell against him and kept on crying.

"I am truly sorry about the *señora,*" Ortez said to Joe in a regretful tone of voice and spreading his hands before him. "But what can I say? You take what you can when you can."

Owens helped Mrs. Dorthea Claxton over to a bench in front of one of the shacks and got her a drink of water from the barrel. She kept her head lowered while the Mexicans began unloading the wagons. It didn't take long with the six men working.

"You are free to go whenever you wish," Ortez said, shrugging his shoulders. "Again I am sorry Señora Claxton had to find out about her husband this way."

The guns had been stored in the smaller shack

and would probably be loaded on horses later in the day or tomorrow. At any rate, Joe knew they would be gone this time tomorrow.

Knowing that there was no reason to wait around for anything, Joe walked over and stood in front of Dorthea Claxton until she looked up at him. Her eyes were red-rimmed and swollen.

"Mrs. Claxton, ma'am," he said in a low sympathetic voice, "we've got to go. It's getting late. We've lost a lot of time."

Mrs. Major Dorthea Claxton, who was probably not so proud of being a major's wife now, wiped her face on the hem of her dress and followed Joe over to the wagon. By the time he mounted Sarge, Boss Owens was up on his wagon.

Once again they headed toward Las Cruces. Only this time the wagons were much lighter and there was a different mission in their minds.

Chapter VI

It took about two miles for Dorthea Claxton to regain her composure and get back some of her zip. She'd been quiet and the few times that Joe had looked back at her driving the wagon he thought she'd been crying. He decided it was best to just leave her alone for a while and let her sort out her own thoughts.

Joe was bothered with his own thoughts. Should he have put up a fight with Ortez for the Gatling guns? Common sense and good judgment told him that it would have been a losing battle with him on the wrong side. He couldn't have done much anyway since Malito had his Colt .45.

But that wasn't the only thing on his mind. Was Ortez lying about a deal he had with Major Edward Claxton? If Ortez hadn't gotten the guns away from them, how much would he have paid Claxton? Or had he already paid him? Why did Claxton have a deal with Ortez in the first place? Was this the first time?

"Yoo hoo, Mr. Howard." Dorthea Claxton's voice was back to its normal volume and broke into his thoughts. He stopped Sarge and waited for her to reach him. He knew immediately from the pinched look on her face and blazing fire in her green eyes that she was through crying and feeling sorry for herself. He would hate like the devil to be in Major Edward Claxton's boots. He decided to ride on the wagon with her for a while and stepped over on it as it was still moving and tied the reins to the brake stick.

"Do you believe everything that Mexican said about Edward?" she asked, dropping the reins to let the horses plod along.

"Well, he seemed to know what he was talking about," Joe answered, resting his elbows on his knees and leaning forward to rest his back. "He knew who you were," he pointed out, turning to look at her. "He knew about Harlon. So I would imagine that he was telling the truth about the rest of it. What are you going to do?"

Dorthea Claxton pressed her mouth into a thin tight line and her eyes were still snapping. She was probably considering her options from the way she shifted her eyes back and forth.

"Isn't it against the law for Edward to give guns to those men?" she asked, a frown pulling two lines between her eyes.

"No, not really," Joe answered, shaking his head slowly. "But then I guess it would depend on why Ortez wanted the guns. You said the major bought them in San Antonio." She nodded and he continued. "Legally they were his to do with what he wanted. Actually the only law that was broken as far as I can tell was when Ortez and his men took the guns from us."

"What do you suppose this Ortez is going to do with so many Gatling guns?" she asked, looking at him sideways.

"It was plain to see that he wasn't a soldier," Joe pointed out a little snidely, and arching his brows. "He's probably going to use them in some kind of revolution. Bassett said there was always some kind of one going on in Mexico."

Joe looked over at Dorthea Claxton and knew immediately that she wasn't believing a word of what he said. It didn't even sound believable to him.

"Did your husband say anything about what he was going to do with the guns before he left you in San Antonio?" Joe asked, thinking of another angle.

"He only said he knew a man in San Antonio who was from New Orleans," Dorthea Claxton answered, expelling a deep and aggravated breath, "who had some Gatling guns. He said the fort could use the guns as added protection against Indian raids. You've got to know," she glared at him and jerked her head, "that he wouldn't tell me and Harlon about anything that was illegal. He's a major in the U.S. Army!"

In Joe's mind he could see a tall man in a military uniform meeting with Ortez somewhere out in the desert and making a deal over a bunch of guns for any number of reasons and for any amount of money.

"What do you think your husband will do?" Joe asked, standing up and pulling Sarge closer to the wagon, "when he finds out that Ortez already has the guns?"

"If someone had something that belonged to you," she countered, arching her brows, "what would you do?"

Joe swung his right leg gingerly over the side of the wagon and eased down on the saddle. He always felt more comfortable and at ease when the big black horse was under him.

"If someone had something of mine," Joe mimicked, looking up at her and grinning, "I'd turn the whole dadblame country upside down until I found them."

A cunning smile spread across Dorthea Claxton's face. "The major just might ask you and Boss Owens to go with him after those guns."

"I'll give it some thought," Joe muttered, wheeling Sarge away from her to head over to Owens.

"What's on yer mind, boy?" Owens asked, sending a stream of tobacco juice over the opposite side of the wagon. "I can almost hear yer brain rompin' 'round inside yer head."

"Well," Joe drew out, pushing his hat back on his head, "Ortez tells me one thing. Mrs. Major Dorthea Claxton tells me something else."

"If Claxton bought them guns," Owens began, spitting again, "they was his to do with what he wanted. If Ortez paid him for half, he was only entitled to half."

The old man's logic coincided with what Joe had told Mrs. Dorthea Claxton. But something just didn't set right in Joe's mind. But suddenly a staggering thought hit Joe. Had the major planned for all of the guns to fall into Ortez's hands? Did he think that something would happen to his wife and son?

No, he admonished, shaking his head rapidly. He was really letting his imagination run away with him. Why would Claxton want something to happen to his family?

The fort at Las Cruces finally came into view as they topped a ridge and started down. It wasn't like the one at Fort Davis, Texas. Instead of being surrounded by mountains like the one in Texas, this one was out in the wide open with a view for miles and miles around.

The half adobe and half log walled fort would have been a welcome sight as the sun began dropping down in the sky if he didn't have to tell Major Edward Claxton about the guns.

"Wait a minute," he scolded in a voice so low that he could hardly hear it himself. "Those guns weren't my responsibility. I got Mrs. Major Dorthea Claxton here. That was the deal. It'll be up to her to tell Claxton what happened to the guns."

The wagons finally rolled through the high pole gates and the noise of so many horses brought out soldiers and citizens alike.

"Let's stop at the major's office first," Dorthea Claxton said, heading her wagon in that direction. She pulled the horses to a stop and Joe had to hurry to get to the wagon to help her down.

Dorthea Claxton's face was pale then turned red as she and Joe hurried up the two steps in front of the major's office. A young blond headed corporal jumped to his feet when he saw her.

"It's good to see you, ma'am," he said in a high pitched voice. "The major thought you'd be here yesterday. Hope nothin' bad happened to you."

Dorthea Claxton jerked around to look at Joe and shook her head quickly. Joe would gladly let her do the talking.

"Where is Edward?" she asked, starting toward the closed door.

"Oh, he and a patrol rode out early this morning," the corporal answered, shrugging his thin shoulders. "Somethin' about some Indians causin' some trouble."

A knot pulled tight in Joe's stomach and the hairs felt like they were standing straight out on the back of his neck. Was this patrol connected in some way with the guns and Ortez and his men? Something told Joe that it did and he would be surprised if he was proven wrong.

Relieved and feeling that his job was over, Joe needed a breath of fresh air and went outside. Boss Owens was leaning against the wagon wheel, a disgruntled frown on his face.

"What's the matter, Boss?" Joe asked, walking up to him and slapping him on the shoulder. "Why do you look so down in the dumps? You should be happy. We're through here. You can go back to Fort Davis. Or," he smiled deviously at Owens, "we can go on out to California. I hear the Barbary Coast has everything that a man could want. We could leave in the morning." Joe wiggled his brows up and down suggestively.

"What do you mean 'California'?" Dorthea Claxton's high pitched voice asked behind him. She'd followed him out on the porch and stood with her hands on her hips. "You can't leave for California. I'd like for you to wait until the major gets back. He'll want to know all about those Mexicans and the guns. There are probably things you could tell him that I've forgotten."

Joe doubted that very much. Dorthea Claxton could probably remember the first dress they put on her the day she was born. When Joe looked around at her he couldn't believe he was seeing the same woman he'd met at Fort Davis a few days ago. Her shoulders slumped and there was a desolate, hurt expression in her green eyes.

For the third time, the others being when Harlon died and when she'd found out that Claxton was dealing with the Mexicans, Joe felt sorry for Dorthea Claxton. Shrugging his shoulders, he decided that one more day wouldn't make that much difference.

"Okay," he agreed, expelling a deep breath and glancing at Boss. The old man smiled at him. "Let's get these horses unhitched."

Joe and Boss gathered up the reins and started leading the horses toward the corral. A soldier wearing sergeant's stripes on his blue shirt was sitting on the top rail polishing the barrel of a Winchester rifle. An obviously new hat was perched at an arrogant angle on his red head. Eyes that reminded Joe of blue ice raked over him in a slow dissecting way.

"Don't tell me you've already unloaded those guns," the sergeant said in a sarcastic voice, cocking a brow and pulling his full mouth into a sneering smile.

"No, as a matter of fact," Joe began, looking down at the ground then slowly raising his eyes to meet the blue ones, "we had some unexpected help . . ."

Joe was interrupted when the sergeant jumped down and leaned the rifle against the corral. From the sullen expression on the man's face, Joe knew he didn't want to hear any excuses or explanations. For some reason this sergeant had a grudge against Joe and there was going to be only one way to settle it.

"I told Major Claxton that I should have gone

along with him and bring the guns back," the sergeant said, hooking his thumbs over his belt and walking a half circle around Joe and back again. "But he said his wife and son could get somebody on the way back from San Antonio."

The sergeant stopped talking, faced Joe and looked him squarely in the eye. He and Joe were the same height but the sergeant had about twenty pounds on Joe. His face was only inches from Joe's. It was then that Joe got a good whiff of the man's breath. There was no doubt about it! The man had been drinking and maybe the liquid courage was one reason why he was acting the way he did.

"Hey, look," Joe said pensively, holding up his hands defensively and taking a step backward. "I don't want any trouble with you. We don't have the guns. Mrs. Claxton will explain all of that to the major when he gets back. Then he can tell anybody he wants to. All I want to do is unhitch these horses, take a bath and get a cup of coffee."

The sergeant threw back his head and a laugh that really sounded like a shout burst from his throat. Before Joe knew it or could do anything about it the soldier drew back his fist and smiling as he did it, planted it squarely in Joe's face.

Joe tasted blood as his mouth was smashed in against his teeth. He staggered back, losing his hat, surprised by the unexpected blow. He fell against the horses. That was all that kept him from going down.

Joe regained his balance and glanced over at Boss. One part of him wanted the old soldier to do something but the other part didn't. He wouldn't feel like much of a man if someone, especially someone older than he, had to help him fight his battle. But glancing back hurriedly at the drunken soldier, Joe knew that he had just enough liquor in him that it would be hard to beat him.

The other soldiers gathering around knew enough not to mix in on someone else's fight. Joe knew it was between him and this drunk with the injured pride. He ducked as the sergeant took another swing at him. The force of the swing took the man half way around but in defiance of his inebriated state and the law of gravity, he managed to keep his balance and faced Joe, a murderous glare in his blue eyes.

"You're going to regret the minute you laid your eyes on me," the sergeant predicted, a snarl on his thin lips. Joe suddenly realized that if he hadn't smelled the whiskey on the man's breath he wouldn't have been able to tell that he'd been drinking by his speech.

"I already do," Joe replied complacently. Doubling up his right fist Joe drew back and landed it on the man's chin. It didn't budge him!

Joe couldn't believe his eyes. He had put all he had into the punch. It should have at least taken him back a couple of steps. All it did was loosen the new hat from the man's red head. It came off and landed on the ground a few inches from Joe's feet. The soldier blinked his eyes a couple of times and smiled maliciously.

"You've got to do better than that, boy," he advised sarcastically, wagging his head from side to side and grinning.

"Okay, I will," Joe answered through tightly clenched teeth. He wished he hadn't done that. His mouth was beginning to smart. But the insult of being called a boy by this drunk lit a raging fire in Joe. It hadn't bothered him when Boss Owens called him "boy." But this was entirely different.

Something told Joe that hitting the sergeant above the shoulders wouldn't get it done. So stepping back half a pace, Joe drew back his right fist again and, putting all of his strength into it again, slammed it into the man's middle. Joe was luckier this time. The blow doubled the sergeant over, leaving his square jawed chin exposed. Joe brought his hands together, lacing the fingers and swung with all of his strength from the left.

The blow straightened the sergeant up and he seemed to hang suspended where he stood. Joe drew back and let him have another blow in the stomach as hard as he could. The air swooshed out of the sergeant's gaping mouth and he fell over backward in the red powdery dust. He lay there trying to pull a ragged breath into his lungs. Joe stood over him, breathing hard and rubbing his knuckles. He spat out a mouth full of blood.

"I guess ye showed him," Boss yelled out, grinning and slapping his hands down against his thighs. "He needed to be taken down a few pegs."

"I didn't see you swinging any licks," Joe snapped, frowning over at the old man. Joe's mouth felt as big as a shovel.

"His fight was with ye, not me," Boss pointed out through squinting eyes, sending a stream of tobacco juice down between his feet.

"He's not so bad," Joe said, laughing when he saw the amused expression on Boss's face. "His feelings were a little ruffled for some cause and he'd drunk too much. This should help him cool off a little."

Still grinning Joe bent over, grabbed the prone soldier by the front of his blue shirt and dragged him over to the water trough right outside the corral. Picking him up by the belt and front of the shirt Joe dropped him into the water with a sobering splash. The soaking wet man came up sputtering and swearing.

Joe was ready for the man this time. He stepped back from the water trough, drew the Colt .45 and aimed it at the sergeant struggling to climb out of the water.

"What in the devil is going on here?" a loud voice called out sharply from behind them. Joe whirled around and saw a squat built man in a major's uniform standing with Dorthea Claxton in front of the office. Joe knew he had to be Major Edward Claxton and was nothing as he'd expected him to be. He weighed at least a hundred and eighty pounds. He was fat. "O'Connor, get up here. The two of you," he pointed at Joe and Boss, "get up here right now."

Joe could tell from the harsh sound in his voice that he was used to giving orders. Joe holstered the pistol, then he and Boss started walking back across the parade ground. O'Connor, wringing water out of his hat, pushed his stringy red wet hair back out of his face. When the three men reached the office Joe and Boss stepped up on the porch by Dorthea Claxton. O'Connor stood at rigid attention before the major.

"Just what was the meaning of that?" Claxton asked, inclining his head toward the corral, a dark frown on his tanned face. His gray eyes snapped and he was breathing so hard and fast that the buttons on his blue coat were at the point of bursting.

"Oh, there was just a little misunderstanding," Joe began lightly, trying to take the edge off the situation. He didn't see any point in any of them getting into trouble.

"Like what?" Claxton snapped, his eyes boring into Joe. He removed his hat from a round head with plastered down black hair and wiped his face with a white handkerchief. "I don't tolerate fighting here at the fort. I want to know exactly what it was all about." He put the handkerchief back into his pants pocket.

Joe lowered his head and leveled a look at the major. It was easy to see why Mrs. Major Dorthea Claxton acted the way she did. She'd been married to this pompous man too long and some of his ways had rubbed off on her.

"This here sergeant thought he shoulda done what Joe did," Boss put in, a disgusted frown on his face. "He had a little too much to drink and jumped Joe at the corral. He thinks you done him wrong."

Major Edward Claxton's face turned a brilliant red and he pressed his lips together so tightly that a white line formed around them. Apparently he wasn't used to any back talk.

"Do you know who you're talking to?" Claxton asked shortly, glaring at Boss. Joe knew the man wished he was taller so he could have looked down his nose at Boss.

"He's well aware of who he's talking to," Joe answered coldly and drawing the words out, shifting his weight from one foot to the other. There was no way he was going to let this glory-hungry piece of humanity talk to the old man like this. "Boss

Owens has been in the army for more years than you've had those major stripes on your fat shoulders."

A pleased feeling eased over Joe as he watched the color drain from Major Edward Claxton's face and his chest swelled as he drew in a harsh breath. Claxton started to say something but Joe beat him to it.

"You asked a question," Joe went on, knowing he was in trouble and wanting to hit Claxton so hard he could taste it, "he answered it."

"Edward," Dorthea Claxton interrupted in a tired voice, "it doesn't matter who's talking to who. I've already explained to you about Harlon and the guns. Harlon's death was more or less to be expected. He'd been sick for a long time. But we weren't expecting to lose the guns to those Mexicans. You've tried to tell me one story in that Ortez only knew the guns were coming here and took them. Ortez told something entirely different. He said he'd made a deal with you for half of the guns. I want you to tell Mr. Howard and Mr. Owens and me again, exactly what you were going to do with those guns. I want to know that I didn't burn my and Harlon's things and the stage for nothing. I think you owe Mr. O'Connor an explanation, too."

It was easy to see that Major Edward Claxton wasn't used to being talked to like this in front of others and no doubt in particular by a woman, even if she was his wife. But he'd probably never seen his wife this mad before. Her green eyes were snapping and her mouth was pulled into a tight line.

"Well, not everybody has to know about how inept this scout was," Claxton cut in.

Joe had just about all of the insults he wanted in

one day. Without giving any thought to what he was doing or what the consequences would be, Joe lunged at Claxton, doubled up his fist and let Claxton have it right in the center of his fat face.

Claxton, slapping his hand over his mouth where blood was trickling out, staggered backward and landed in a straight backed wooden chair. Needless to say Claxton was as surprised by the unexpected attack as Joe. He sat there in stunned silence. Claxton stared down at the floor then with his right hand pressed tightly against his face he brought his eyes up to meet Joe's. If looks could kill, Joe just died. Before Joe knew what was happening, Claxton drew in a deep breath and yelled: "Guards!" at the top of his lungs.

Before Joe could spit two soldiers appeared seemingly from out of nowhere and grabbed him roughly by the arms. The one on Joe's right jerked the Colt .45 from the holster and put it in his belt.

"Put that man in the guard house!" Claxton bellowed at the top of his lungs, pulling himself up from the chair.

The two soldiers, like two wooden puppets, pulled Joe down the two steps, almost dragged him bodily across the parade ground, pushed him roughly into a small cell and slammed the iron door shut behind him.

Joe had been in jail only once before in his life. That's when he'd been mistaken for someone else in Pecos, Texas. That situation was a little more serious than this. He could have been hanged in Pecos on false arrest for a rape charge.

This could only get him a stint in the guard house for a long time. But for some reason he didn't feel too worried about this. Just as he was being hustled down the steps in front of the major's office he took a glance back over his shoulder. He caught a look in Mrs. Major Dorthea Claxton's green eyes that told him his troubles would be over soon. But something else told him that he would only be exchanging one kind of trouble for another.

True to his expectation, in less than twenty minutes, although he would swear that it was at least an hour, one of the two soldiers who'd brought him to the cell, wearing a sheepish grin, unlocked the cell door and threw it wide open.

"You're free to go," he said, wrinkling up his forehead.

"What happens now?" Joe asked, taking his pistol from the amused looking soldier and shoving it down in the holster.

"Ah," the soldier said, sucking his teeth in against his mouth, "it appears that the old man," he stopped, coughed and cleared his throat, "had a change of mind or heart and wants to see you."

"Is he still in his office?" Joe asked, walking in long dusty strides with the soldier back across the parade ground. He couldn't begin to imagine what Major Edward Claxton would want to see him about now other than to tell him to hurry and leave the fort.

"Yeah," the soldier answered, nodding his head slowly, that same puzzling smile on his face. "Mrs. Major Claxton is with him." Apparently the young man had had a run in with the major's wife and she'd told him exactly how she wanted to be addressed. Joe remembered his own instructions well.

That was a long time ago, it seemed, and Joe knew he'd hate the "old gal" forever. But a lot had changed his feelings toward her. She really wasn't all that bad. He smiled to himself and shook his head.

The soldier turned to walk away but glanced back at Joe. "You lucky devil," he said, then threw back his head and roared in laughter. Joe guessed it was something he'd wanted to do from the time he'd come to release him from the cell. Boss Owens was sitting on the porch in a rocking chair, a chaw of tobacco in his jaw and whittling on a stick with a thin pocket knife.

"Wonder what he meant by that," Joe mumbled under his breath and frowning, stomping up the same steps he'd been almost dragged down less than half an hour ago.

"You'll find out," Boss answered, leaning forward to send a stream of tobacco juice to the ground. He grinned and wiped the back of his hand across his mouth.

Joe paused outside the door and knocked.

"Come in," the gruff voice bellowed. It belonged unmistakably to Major Edward Claxton. The tone was angry. Joe wondered how Claxton would act toward him since he'd belted him? When Joe opened the door he got an inkling why Claxton sounded as he did. He was sitting behind an oak desk as well arranged as Colonel Eric McRaney's back at Fort Davis.

In fact, the entire office was well arranged. A territorial map with tacks denoting Indian camps covered the entire wall at the end of the office. A U.S. flag and a blue and white fort flag were on either side of a safe at the other end of the office. Two open windows let in the sage scented breeze and evening sun.

Major Edward Claxton sat behind the neat desk in a swivel chair, a sullen scowl on his bruised face.

His mouth was tight or as tight as the swelling would allow and a hard knot worked in his jaws. Claxton's gray eyes were as icy as before. He gripped his hands on top of the desk.

Mrs. Major Dorthea Claxton was sitting in a chair beside the desk facing the door, a complacent smile on her mouth. Joe glanced at her and quickly guessed that her presence had a little something to do with his release and a lot to do with Claxton's appearance and attitude. The smile softened her features but her eyes were narrow and calculating.

"You wanted to see me, sir?" Joe asked, skepticism and suspicion in his voice. He took off his hat and pushed his hair back.

"Yes," Claxton snapped, glaring up at Joe. "Sit down." He indicated the straight backed chair across the desk with a flick of his hand.

Joe sat down in the chair and crossed his legs. If Claxton was going to hurry his departure from the fort surely he wouldn't offer him a seat unless he had a strange sense of humor.

"My wife," he began and inclined his head toward Dorthea Claxton, "told me again and in more depth what happened to the guns." His words were crisp and clipped. "All of the guns were supposed to have come here to the fort and then Ortez was to get his half after he paid me."

That was the same thing Ortez had told Joe earlier in the day so he knew that the Mexican wasn't lying. Joe wondered what Claxton had told his wife earlier.

"Why does Ortez and his men need so many guns, and Gatling guns at that?" Joe asked shrewdly. He was beginning to believe that what Dorthea Claxton had told him earlier was going to happen. He was glad now that he had hit Claxton. He had made a deal with the Mexican for the guns and had endangered his wife and son's life in doing so.

"Oh, there's a revolution of some sort going on down in Mexico all the time," Claxton answered almost evasively and waving his hand again, shifting his eyes from Joe over to his wife and back to Joe again. "I don't care what Ortez does with his guns. But I want my half of the guns back!" Claxton pressed his mouth into a thin line, winced in pain and breathed hard through flared nostrils.

Here it comes, Joe told himself with an inward smile. Claxton is going to ask me to go after the guns. Or better yet, he's going to order me to go after them. He still thinks it's my fault that Ortez got all of the guns.

Claxton looked at Joe for a long time then took and exhaled a long breath. He relaxed, leaned back in the chair and slowly ran his left index finger up and down his short nose. All the while his gray eyes never left Joe's face.

"Do you suppose you could find the place where Ortez and his men stopped you?" Claxton asked sarcastically, a calculating gleam replacing the stoniness in his eyes.

Joe knew beyond a shadow of a doubt that Dorthea Claxton had forced the major to release him from the guard house. In a roundabout way it was Claxton's fault that he was there.

If Claxton hadn't made a deal with Ortez, the Mexican wouldn't have been there to take the guns. All of the guns would have been on the wagon when they reached the fort. O'Connor wouldn't have had any reason to jump him and Joe wouldn't have tied into the major because of an insult.

Joe also realized that he could make one of two choices. He knew Claxton wanted him to take him back to the place where Ortez got the guns. Joe could either take him there and he and Boss could be on their way to wherever, or he could refuse and spend a couple of months in the guard house. But he wasn't going to let Claxton off that easy.

"Sure," he answered pragmatically and shrugging his shoulders. "All you've got to do is ride out the gate, turn left on the trail and head east. It's simple."

Claxton wasn't at all amused with Joe's suggestion. He slammed his fist down on the desk and jumped to his feet. His face was crimson and his gray eyes bulged at Joe. "Then you shouldn't have any trouble in finding the place, should you?" he shouted, leaning forward to drive home his point.

"No, I guess not," Joe agreed, arching his brows. "But," he held up his hand to ward off any arguments from Claxton, "there's no point in starting out before morning. Boss and I are too tired to go today and besides it's too late."

Claxton must have seen the merit of Joe's suggestion because he nodded slowly in agreement. "We'll leave about sunup."

Dorothea Claxton had been silent all this time. But now she fluttered her hands across her dress as if brushing off dust and stood up. Then she did something that Joe would have sworn he'd never see her do. She smiled broadly and winked at him with her right eye. The major wouldn't have seen her do it anyway because he was looking down at his desk and shuffling through a stack of papers.

"Well," she said, as Joe stood up and replaced his

hat, “I'm going to take a bath, change clothes and try out my new white horse. I might decide to go with you tomorrow and ride her.”

“I can just see the major letting you go with us tomorrow,” Joe said, a frown pulling his brows together and a half smile on his mouth.

“I can just see him trying to stop me,” Dorthea Claxton replied flatly, a cunning smirk on her mouth. “Edward still has a lot more explaining to do. And until I'm completely satisfied with his explanations, he's not about to tell me what I can and can't do.” A spiteful grin and a hard look in her green eyes told Joe that she meant every word she said.

Joe could understand why she was talking and acting the way she was. Dorthea Claxton felt that the major had put her in undue danger by letting her bring guns so far when half of them belonged to a bandit. He hadn't known that Quintin and Daniels would happen along with a deal of their own with the Indian Chee Two Hats. She probably felt that she'd kept the guns from falling into the wrong hands by herself with a little help from Joe and Boss only to lose them so close to the fort because of him.

Joe noticed that Dorthea Claxton was treating him with a lot more civility and he felt good about it. With her in her present vindictive mood against her husband he didn't want to be on her wrong side and he didn't envy the major at all.

“We're going after those guns in the morning,” Joe said to the questioning look on Boss's face when he came out of the office.

Joe and Boss started across the parade ground to the mess hall while Dorthea Claxton turned toward the small white adobe cottage.

"The 'old gal', as you call her," Joe said, watching Dorthea Claxton walking away from them swinging her arms like she had done when he'd first met her at Fort Davis, "is really something."

"Why?" Boss asked, a wistfulness in his voice and eyes.

"I don't know what happened before I got out of the guard house," Joe began, a wide smile on his face, "but she must have given the major the devil. He didn't look too pleased about anything that was going on. But I got the impression that if I don't want to spend some more time in the guard house, you and I have to show the major where we lost the guns."

Joe was surprised when Boss caught him by the left arm and swung him around to face him. "Lost the guns?" he repeated, raising his voice. "What do ye mean, 'lost the guns'? Didn't she tell him that them Mexicans took 'um?"

"Yeah, she told him," Joe answered, pulling his arm free and walking on to the mess hall. Boss followed him in when he opened the door. "And I told him. But he'd only give so much."

Six soldiers were sitting at one of two long tables in the mess hall. A black pot-bellied stove with a much used coffee pot bubbling off a good smelling aroma was at the west end of the long narrow building. About two dozen blue speckled enamel cups were on a side table. Joe started toward the table and heard a snicker behind him. Spinning around he saw one soldier looking straight at him, his hand covering his mouth.

"Did I miss something?" Joe asked in a level voice, reaching down and picking up a cup. He had a pretty good idea what it was all about. O'Connor was nowhere to be seen.

"Well," the soldier sitting at the end of the table said, looking sideways at his companions, "it's not every day that we get to see a grown man who has to depend on a woman to fight his battles for him."

Joe knew the soldier was goading him. He wanted to chalk it up to the fact that very little excitement happened at the fort and the soldier was just letting off a little steam. But that couldn't be true with so much Indian trouble around and the revolution down in Mexico.

"Why?" Joe asked, hot anger beginning to burn in his stomach, "did someone else come in after me and Boss?" He knew that no one had but he pretended to look around.

"No," the soldier answered, a smug grin on his long face. He shook his head slowly. "Nobody else came in. I was talking about you. We've all heard about what Mrs. Claxton did for you. If it wasn't for her, you'd still be in the guard house. The major should have left you there. You had no call to hit him."

Undoubtedly thinking that Joe would stand there and take these insults, too, a self-righteous smile spread across the soldier's face. The other soldiers laughed along with him and poked each other in the ribs.

Before Joe knew it or could think about what he was doing again, he dropped the cup, covered the short distance between the stove and table in a few steps. Reaching out he grabbed the stunned and wild-eyed youngster by the front of his blue shirt and jerked him up from the bench. The smile froze on the soldier's face and turned into fear. He soon realized from the threatening look in Joe's brown eyes that he was anything but cowardly.

"Look, sonny," Joe growled low in his throat, his face only inches from the other man's, "I don't know who in the devil you've been talking to but apparently he didn't tell you everything."

Knowing he'd probably end up in the guard house again, Joe drew back his right fist and smashed it directly into the soldier's face. His head snapped back, he lost his hat and a cut appeared on his left cheek just below the eye. Still gripping a handful of shirt, Joe drew back again and let him have the sharp blow in the stomach. The breath exploded out of the soldier's lungs and the impact knocked him backward. He tried to regain his balance as he stumbled but one foot caught behind the other and he hit the floor with a thud.

All eyes were on the soldier and he turned a brilliant red as he struggled to his feet. Without saying anything the battered and bedraggled man picked up his hat, clamped it down on his head and hurried from the mess hall.

"Now," Joe said, turning around and taking a deep breath, looked each man straight in the eye, "does anybody else have anything to say?"

Without saying anything each man solemnly shook his head, got up and left. Joe and Boss filled their plates and ate.

The sun had finally slipped down in the sky when Joe and Boss reached the barracks. Joe was hesitant to open the door.

"Wonder if we'll have any trouble in here?" Boss asked, opening the door.

"I hope not," Joe answered, shaking his head wearily. "I don't think my fist can take any more abuse." He flexed his right hand and grimaced in pain.

Oh, God, Joe thought with a sickening feeling when they stepped inside. Ten soldiers sat on their bunks but only glanced up, mostly out of idle curiosity when Joe and Boss walked in. For a wild second Joe thought he'd have to defend himself against at least two of them. But that didn't happen. But he wasn't going to take the chance or waste the time.

"I don't want any trouble from anyone," he began sternly. "All we want is a place to sleep. We'll be gone tomorrow. Just point out two bunks that nobody will fight us for." An anxious feeling sent shivers up and down Joe's back.

"The two bunks at the end are empty," one old grizzled soldier who could have passed for Boss's brother said, pointing to the opposite end of the barracks.

"Thanks," Joe said, relieved that he wasn't going to have to fight any of them. The bunks were on either side of a window and the cool breeze coming through it felt good and he knew they'd sleep well.

They'd forgotten to get their bedrolls and saddlebags but were too tired to go after them now. Joe took off his boots, socks and shirt and stretched out on top of the gray wool blanket. It didn't take long for him to drop off into a deep sleep.

He didn't know how long he'd been sleeping when he was awakened by the need to go answer nature's call. Pulling on his boots he tiptoed across the floor, quietly opened the door and stepped out into the warm night.

After he'd done what he'd come out to do, Joe decided to go by the corral and get his and Boss's bedrolls and saddlebags. He had to pass the tack shed and stopped abruptly when he heard voices coming from inside. They both sounded familiar but he couldn't be sure since they were so muffled. It had to be almost midnight and Joe wondered what kind of business could draw two men out at such a late hour.

As quietly as he could Joe eased up by the door and listened. He didn't expect to hear what came to his ears.

"I never thought you'd do such a boneheaded thing, O'Connor," Major Edward Claxton berated in a sullen voice. "If you hadn't gotten drunk and shot off your mouth to Howard, we wouldn't be in this mess now."

Why was Claxton being so hard on the sergeant, Joe wondered, a funny feeling pulling a knot in his stomach. He frowned and listened harder.

"Now you just hold on a second," O'Connor said in a slow hard voice. "If I'd gone along on this trip to bring the guns back like I have on the other trips, this 'mess' as you call it, wouldn't have happened."

What other buying trips for guns, Joe asked himself, while chills raced up and down his naked back. If there had been other buying trips why hadn't Dorthea Claxton gone along. Why hadn't O'Connor been on this trip?

"O'Connor, if you had an ounce of sense in your head, your hat wouldn't fit," Claxton accused in a tight voice. "It would have looked strange if you'd gone along with Dorthea and Harlon this time. It would have been implying that Harlon couldn't handle things. He felt a lot better and I thought the trip would be good for him. How in the devil did I know he was going to die?"

It was all Joe could do to stand still and listen to all of this. There was no remorse at all in Major Edward Claxton's voice over the death of his son. How long had he been buying guns for Ortez's revolution?

"Well, if I'd been along," O'Connor shot back, rage in his voice, "Mrs. Claxton wouldn't have needed a scout."

"Keep your voice down," the major cautioned, expelling a disgruntled hiss.

"Well, tell me again how it is my fault," O'Connor asked, pique in his voice.

"If you hadn't picked a fight with Howard," Claxton explained in a tired voice, "I wouldn't have had to break it up. Howard wouldn't have hit me for insulting him and ended up in the guard house."

There was a long pause before Claxton continued: "Somehow Dorthea has taken a liking to him and thinks there's something strange about the gun deal with Ortez. She's made me agree to let him take me to the place where Ortez took the guns. I'm surprised she didn't come up with the idea of Howard and that old man going over into Mexico after Ortez and the guns."

Joe heard them moving around inside and quickly stepped around the corner out of sight. Claxton and O'Connor emerged from the tack shed and went their separate ways. Joe watched them as a diabolical plan formed in his mind and a malicious smile eased slowly across his face. He wondered if Claxton had explained things to his wife's satisfaction?

Hurrying back to the barracks Joe eased over to Boss. The old soldier was snoring loud enough to awaken the dead. Joe touched him lightly on the shoulder and hoped that he'd awaken quietly. Owens moaned low, rolled over and opened his eyes.

"What's the matter?" he mumbled, rubbing his hand over his face.

"Get up and follow me outside," Joe said, bending down to whisper in his ear. Owens pulled his boots on and, stumbling over his own feet followed Joe outside. They walked a good way from the barracks and when Joe explained his idea to Boss the old man threw back his head and roared in laughter. Joe was surprised when the troops didn't come tearing out of the barracks.

"When ye tell the major ye want to go to Mexico and get them guns," Owens finally said, when he regained his composure and drew in a deep breath and cleared his throat, "that man is goin' to bust a blood vessel. He's got a sweet set-up goin' with that Ortez. He probably charges him as much for his half of the guns as he paid for all of 'um. Ortez is so glad to get the guns that he don't say anythin'."

"Maybe he doesn't know it," Joe said laughing and slapping Owens on the shoulder. "Something tells me that all of that is about to come to an end."

Chapter VII

Joe was awakened early the next morning by the troops stomping out of the barracks when the reveille bugle sounded before daylight. As fast as he could Joe put on clean underwear, pants, shirt and pulled on his boots. Boss could probably sleep through a cattle stampede unless the cattle ran directly over him. He was still snoring, his mouth wide open and his arm over his forehead.

"Boss, wake up," Joe called out, shaking the old man's shoulders. "It's time to eat." They could hear the cook banging on the triangle outside the mess hall. "Then it will be time to go."

Anxiety and anticipation took turns sending goose bumps up and down Joe's back as he and Boss walked toward the mess hall. All heads turned their direction when they entered. The soldier who had been on the receiving end of Joe's fist yesterday glared at Joe and touched the red cut under his eye. O'Connor came in, looking as battered as the other soldier, filled his cup with strong black coffee and sat down at the far end of the table.

Joe only glanced his way then turned his full attention to a platter of fried eggs, ham and biscuits on the side table. He forked three eggs, a thick slice of ham and two golden brown biscuits onto a tin plate, filled a cup with scalding hot black coffee and sat down at the opposite end of the table away from any of the soldiers in case they wanted to started anything with him. Boss dropped down on the bench by him, his own plate similarly laden except he had only two eggs.

"Do ye suppose the old gal is really going with us?" Boss asked, taking a long sip of coffee and looking at Joe, a gleam in his eyes.

"Boss, you still beat all," Joe said, swallowing a mouth full of eggs and bread. "The 'old gal' is married," Joe stressed, frowning dubiously at the old man. Boss looked remorseful and Joe actually felt sorry for him. He seemed to have it bad for the major's wife. "Okay, Boss, let your mind go. If the major wasn't around what would you have to offer her?"

A sly grin crept over Boss' face and he ducked his head in a mild pretense of embarrassment. "Oh, I don't know," he finally acknowledged, "but it would be fun to spend some time with her. Like I said. She's like somethin' I never seen before."

No more was said while the two men wolfed down their breakfasts and drank three cups of coffee each. When they'd finally finished eating they stacked their plates and cups and Boss took them to the kitchen while Joe went back to the barracks and gathered up their saddlebags and bedrolls.

Boss was waiting for Joe at the corral when he walked up. The sun was up high enough for Joe to see Owens's face. He was leaning nonchalantly against the corral, holding the reins for Sarge and his own horse and grinning from ear to ear. Joe didn't have to ask why Boss looked so happy. All he had to do was turn around and look toward the major's white adobe cottage. He didn't believe what he saw.

The white horse that had belonged to the Indian Chee Two Hats only two days ago was tied to the hitch rail in front of the cottage. He sported a McClelland saddle instead of a sidesaddle as Joe had expected. Joe was really surprised at this. It was considered unladylike for a woman of Mrs. Major Dorthea Claxton's position in life to ride astride. Apparently she was breaking all of the rules of propriety now and starting to do things the way she wanted. Or was she just spiting the major? An extra horse, a sorrel mare was also saddled. Joe reasoned that it was the major's.

Joe went up the steps and was just about to knock on the door when it opened. Mrs. Dorthea Claxton stood there, a wide satisfied smile on her face. A wicked grin sparkled in her green eyes. She looked well rested and it was hard to tell from her appearance what she'd endured the past couple of weeks.

"Is that Howard?" Edward Claxton's still irritated voice questioned from behind her. "If it is, tell him to go to the corral and saddle up the pack mule and then go get a grub sack together."

Hot anger shot through Joe and sent a bitter taste into his mouth. The tone in Claxton's voice was more of a master giving orders to a slave.

"Good morning, ma'am," Joe greeted, pushing his hat back and grinning at her. His anger subsided a little at her defiance. "I guess from the way you're dressed, you are going with us."

He never thought he'd see Mrs. Major Dorthea Claxton wearing a pair of black wool pants and a dark blue shirt. Instead of her usual bonnets, she wore a black flat-crowned hat, much like Joe's but a lot better. Her red hair was smoothed straight back from her face and hung in one single braid down her back. Boss is going to have a fit when he sees her now, Joe thought, shaking his head slowly.

"Tell the major that I'm not an errand boy to saddle pack mules," Joe said loud enough for Claxton to hear, "and that I don't put grub sacks together. All I'm supposed to do is show him where Ortez got the guns yesterday." Joe had decided to save his surprise for Claxton until later.

Edward Claxton could have heard Joe's voice if he'd been standing twenty yards away but made no reply. Dorthea Claxton smiled at Joe and shook her head.

"Don't worry about food or a pack mule," she said in a light voice, tightening the leather chin strap. "It's already been taken care of. I had it arranged last night."

Joe was losing more and more respect for Major Edward Claxton and liking the 'old gal' much better. First Claxton had wanted his wife and ill son to bring Gatling guns from San Antonio to Las Cruces. That was a long way for a well person. They had no way of knowing that the major had made a deal with Ortez, a Mexican bandit, for half of the guns. Anything could and did happen between the two points.

Joe knew that Claxton was trying to save face in front of his wife and impress him in going after his half of the guns. But another thing about Claxton: He was trying to get the upper hand on Joe by ordering him around like he was some lackey to get the pack mule and grub sack. He'd lost out on that aspect when his wife had beat him to it.

"If we're all ready," Joe said, turning around and beckoning to Boss to bring the horses, "let's go." Joe was amazed at how little time it took for Boss to cover the distance from the corral to the cottage. He was leading a pack mule with a huge grub sack tied across a wooden rack. He was also leading Sarge and his own horse. He tipped his cap and smiled at Dorthea Claxton. As Joe had suspected the old man's eyes almost fell out of their sockets when he really looked at her. He noticed that the major's wife smiled slightly at the old man.

Major Edward Claxton was in his full major's uniform when he came out of the cottage. A dark blue coat, with gold buttons strained around his rotund body. Lighter blue pants with the legs down in highly polished black boots had a yellow stripe down the side. A blue campaign hat sat squarely on his plastered down hair.

Joe knew the uniform gave the major a more authoritative look and that it was to impress him and Boss. But he also knew that the stripes wouldn't mean anything when they got over into Mexico. Claxton would have no jurisdiction there and only be a citizen like Joe and Boss. Joe wondered why he'd gone to so much trouble.

Claxton swung up on the horse, letting his wife fend for herself. Joe was disgusted at the major's indifference. Boss saw the opportunity to shine more in her eyes and rushed to help her.

"Howard, since you know the way," Claxton said, contempt sharp in his voice and eyes, "why don't you lead out?"

Joe knew this undertaking was going to require a lot of time and hoped that his temper and nerves could endure it. He knew Claxton would be watching every move he made and would no doubt take great pleasure in finding fault with everything he did.

The sun had already crested the eastern sky and had painted the white clouds with touches of red and yellow. A cool breeze put energy into the horses. The four travelers had to stop only twice to rest the animals before reaching the three adobe shacks where Ortez and his five companions had taken the two wagon loads of Gatling guns yesterday.

"I can't understand why you let yourself fall into a trap like that," Claxton accused, standing up in the stirrups and looking around. "You should have suspected something wasn't right when you saw Malito lying on the ground."

The old saying that if a man was given enough rope, he'd hang himself suddenly popped into Joe's mind. Evidently Boss and Dorthea Claxton picked up on it as soon as Joe did. Three pairs of eyes were riveted on Major Edward Claxton and he turned red. "Why are you all looking at me like that?" he questioned in a snappy voice. He knew immediately that he'd made a mistake.

"How did you know that someone named Malito would be with this Ortez?" Dorthea Claxton asked suspiciously, pulling the white horse closer to her husband. She frowned deeply and her green eyes bored into his.

"Major, I heard you and O'Connor talking last night," Joe put in before Claxton could answer his wife. Claxton's face turned white and he took a sharp breath. "How many deals have you had with Ortez? How many guns have you sold to him?"

Claxton eased back down on the saddle and glared at Joe. Then a sneering grin pulled his mouth to one side and he arched his brows. "I don't know what you heard. I don't have to answer any of your questions. It's none of your business. The only reason you're along is to help me get my half of the guns back. Is that clear?"

Dorthea Claxton expelled a disgruntled breath and Joe jerked around on the saddle to look at her. She looked like she wanted to vomit.

"It is his business, Edward," she contradicted, shaking her head disdainfully. "His life, along with mine and Mr. Owens's is on the line here. We could all get killed."

Joe realized that they were wasting time and nothing was going to be gained by asking Major Claxton any more questions. Shaking his head in disgust Joe swung down and walked toward the larger of the three shacks. When he pushed open the rickety door, he half expected to see either Ortez and Malito squatting on the floor with a Gatling gun aimed at him.

He was relieved though, when after looking around the one room building, he saw that it was empty except for a brown tarantula in a corner. The other two shacks were also empty. A smug grin on Claxton's face irritated Joe when he swung up on Sarge.

"Did you find anything?" Claxton asked sarcastically, pushing his blue hat back on his head.

"No," Joe said petulantly, expelling a deep breath, "and you probably knew that I wouldn't." Without waiting for Claxton to answer Joe reined the black horse around to the back of the shack. He wasn't ready for what he saw. All of the boxes which had contained the Gatling guns were in a disassembled heap. Why would Ortez take the guns out of the boxes, Joe was wondering when Boss came around the corner of the shack. No doubt Ortez already had them assembled.

"Do ye think that Mexican was goin' to build a fire to make hisself some tortillas?" Boss asked, pulling his horse up by Joe and grinning.

"No," Joe answered, drawing the word out. He glanced quickly from Owens back to the boxes. He knew instantly what Ortez had done. To prove himself right, Joe urged Sarge around and started to ride a wide circle around the shack, all under the rancorous eye of Major Edward Claxton.

Joe knew there would be no need to ride east. That was the way they'd come yesterday. So that would save him some time. North was out since that was the opposite way they were going. Joe felt like he'd been handed a medal when he rode back to the south side of the shack and took a closer look down at the ground. Four sets of very deep wagon ruts were heading directly south. Judging from the depth of the ruts Joe knew the wagons weren't traveling too fast. That was one good thing in their favor but the bandits did have a day and maybe a night against them.

"Are you thinking what I am?" Joe asked Boss, who'd ridden up by him again and was looking down at the ruts. Boss raised his head and thoughtfully ran his thumb back and forth on his chin.

"Yeah, I believe I am," Boss answered, deep lines forming between his eyes. "Ortez and his men unloaded them Gatling guns and mounted 'um on somethin'."

Once again a helpless sensation rolled over Joe. He felt in a way it was still his fault that Ortez had gotten not only half of the guns which were actually his, but the other half that belonged to Claxton. Joe, as Boss had pointed out, knew the guns were mounted and whoever Ortez was going up against didn't stand a chance. But then a calming thought diminished the helpless feeling.

From what Joe had overheard last night this wasn't the first time Ortez had gotten guns from Claxton. Even if Ortez had only gotten half of the guns he would still be well armed.

"To save ourselves a lot of time following tracks that could split up any time," Joe said, changing his mind about surprising Claxton in going after the guns, "do you have any idea where in Mexico Ortez would go?"

Joe was suffering under the illusion that Major Edward Claxton was a sensible man who'd volunteer some information that would speed things up and possibly save their lives.

But apparently what was sensible to Joe was an unheard of condition to Major Edward Claxton. Joe knew no help would be coming from the major when Claxton took a deep breath and ran his tongue over his upper lip.

"If I'm going to have to help you do your job," Claxton said, pulling himself up proudly, sarcasm narrowing his eyes, "you might as well go back to the fort."

Once again the overwhelming desire to hit Claxton shot through Joe. But before he could do or say anything Dorthea Claxton rode the white horse up by the major and from the disgusted smirk on her face, Joe was glad beyond words that he wasn't in the major's highly polished boots, which were now covered with dust.

"Edward," she said bitterly, "I never thought I'd live to see the day when I'd say this and now isn't the time to say it, but I'm very disappointed in you. I don't know how many other deals you've had with what's his name and I probably never will. But I don't understand why you're being so pigheaded! If you know where these men are heading, for God's sake tell him!"

The harshness in her voice and glare in her green eyes must have gotten through to Claxton. He expelled a deep breath and sagged in the saddle.

"All right," he relented sharply, glancing from her over to Joe, to Owens and back to Joe. "All right. They're across the border in Mexico," he went on, wagging his head from side to side. "Ortez and his men aren't the regular run of the mill bandits. They're working for the Mexican government. They're federales."

Joe's blood ran cold at the word. He knew that Claxton was lying! Federales were supposed to be, in his way of thinking, federal troops or government soldiers. The men he saw yesterday weren't dressed like the federal troops he'd seen once. They wore caps and uniforms, a far cry from the big sombreros and diverse clothing that Ortez and his men wore.

"They're a contingent of Santa Anna's men station in the state of Chihuahua," Claxton went on, switching the reins nervously from one hand to the other.

"How can you sell guns to a dictator?" Joe asked

incredulously, leaning forward and staring at Claxton. "You're a major in the U.S. Army! If it isn't it should be against the law!" Joe would never think of Colonel Eric McRaney doing such a thing, no matter how much money was involved. Joe didn't know what action, if any, could be taken against Claxton, but when all of this was over he was certainly going to find out.

"We're wasting time," Joe said in a flat voice and wheeling the black horse roughly around. He was in a hurry now to get over in Mexico, find Ortez and his men, get Claxton's guns back and be finished with this disheartening mission.

The four people, each engrossed in their own thoughts, rode past Saguaro cactus with their thick green arms reaching up toward the blue sky in supplication for rain. From looking down at the dry ground it was hard to tell that rain had fallen in torrents only two days ago. The moisture had been sucked in almost as quickly as it had come down.

Joe was concentrating on the tracks still visible when Dorthea Claxton pulled the white horse up by him.

"What are we going to do when we find Ortez's camp?" she asked, taking off her hat and pushing her damp red hair back from her flushed face.

"Ma'am," Joe answered, looking at her and shaking his head slowly. "I don't have any idea. I guess we'll just have to play it by ear. But I do think that since this isn't the first time your husband has done business with these men, he should be the one to lead us into the camp. There are only four of us, and, ma'am, I don't know what you're really doing on this trip. You could get killed, you know."

A pinched look crossed her face but she only smiled at him. "I just might end up saving your rear end," Dorthea Claxton said snidely, arching her brows, cocking her head to one side and looking at Joe. He threw back his head and laughed. But then a sobering through struck him. She just might do it at that. Would she do the same for her husband, Joe wondered.

Boss Owens, who'd been a few yards to the right of Joe, rode up by him. They'd been moving along at a slow pace with no definite plan in mind. "I think I'll ride a little way ahead," he said, pulling his cap down tighter on his head. When he took his pistol from the holster, spun the cylinder with a lot less flare than he'd seen Joe use and started toward the hills ahead.

Joe knew that if he didn't follow Boss the old soldier would go ahead on his own. Kneeing Sarge in the side he reached Boss and kept on riding. There was no point in delaying this any longer.

Hills turned into granite mountains that soared up to scrape the blue sky that was becoming overcast. That was one good thing in their favor. It would be cooler and the horses could move faster and they could save some time.

Joe was surprised and relieved when the heavy wagon tracks didn't split up. He knew there were at least six men they were following. The thing that worried him now was he didn't know and Claxton probably wouldn't know either, how many more bandits or federales there were ahead.

The trail wound in and out of the mountains. The four people crossed small streams and rivers. They stopped in the shade of a cholla cactus when the dim sun was overhead and munched on hard-tack and cold fried potatoes, probably from last night. The idea of no fire was Major Claxton's. Joe was pretty sure that they'd already been observed. He didn't think that Ortez was a stupid man. He was sure that if he had something that belonged to the Mexican, like the guns, Ortez would come after them.

After eating they started out once again. The terrain was much as it had been earlier in the day. In and out of ravines. Around and over hills. Around mountains that dwarfed any that Joe had ever seen. The mountains gave way to desert with fuzzy topped cactus.

They rode until the sun began easing down in the sky and painting it purple. All four of them were dismayed that the only sign of Ortez and his men were the still visible wagon ruts.

It wasn't quite dark when they found a water hole with a few trees around it. Joe was disgusted, tired and hungry. He didn't care if a fire brought out every Indian or bandit in the mountains. Claxton didn't say anything when Joe called a stop for the night. In fact, he unsaddled his and his wife's horses and even unloaded the pack mule and laid out the bedrolls. But when he saw Joe gathering up wood for a fire he started trying to act like a major again.

"What in the devil do you think you're doing?" Claxton snapped, glaring down at Joe, his hands on his hips.

"What does it look like?" Joe shot back, dropping the wood on the ground then squatting down to light the fire. "We've been riding all day. We haven't seen a living soul. I don't know about Mrs.

Claxton or Boss, or you for that matter. But I'm hungry and I'll be danged if I'm going to settle for jerky and cold potatoes tonight. If Ortez and his men get us, at least I'll have a full stomach."

The major started to argue with him but Dorthea Claxton interrupted. "Mr. Howard is right. Some real food would be good for all of us."

"A cup of coffee would taste good," Boss put in, taking the coffee pot from the grub sack and filling it from the water hole. He smiled at Dorthea Claxton, put grounds in the pot and set it on the fire.

Dorthea Claxton opened a can of beans and sliced off salt pork while Joe made bread. He was sure he'd starve to death until he could eat as the combined aromas assaulted his senses.

"We're all going to regret this," Claxton said, shaking his head dejectedly. Nevertheless, he accepted a plate with beans, bread and meat and a cup of coffee from his wife. The plate was cleaned almost as fast as Joe's.

By the time the four people had finished eating and cleaning up the dishes, long shadows were reaching eastward and the land was a lot cooler. They spread their bedrolls on the ground. Joe was surprised when Dorthea Claxton, as though she'd done it many times before, rolled out her own blankets and dropped down on them with a deep sigh. She looked tired and deep lines were etched around her mouth.

For a while everything was quiet, then the sounds of the night took over. A dove cooed in a nearby cactus. Crickets sang their song in the grass by the water hole. Up in the mountains they heard a sound like a woman crying.

"Is that another cry of the ghosts?" Dorthea Claxton asked Joe, sitting up and peering closer at him in the darkness. He could almost see the joking gleam in her green eyes.

"What ghosts are you talking about?" Major Edward Claxton asked before Joe could answer, a snide tone in his voice. His blanket was on the opposite side of his wife's. He had to sit all the way up, look past her and try to see Joe. "That was only a mountain lion and you know it."

"Oh, that was a little joke that Joe played on Dor . . . on Mrs. Claxton the first night away from the fort," Boss Owens called out on Joe's right side. Joe noticed how he'd almost called Dorthea Claxton by her first name and caught himself. Joe wondered if the major would care. Somehow he doubted it.

"Why is it, Owens," Claxton asked irritably, "when I direct a question to Howard, you always answer it for him?" Joe couldn't see Claxton too clearly in the dimness but from their other encounters he could visualize a snarl on the major's mouth and a frown between his eyes.

"Oh, Edward," Dorthea Claxton scoffed, expelling a disgusted sigh, "for heaven's sake, don't be such a stuffed shirt. Mr. Owens was only putting in his two cents worth. We're all entitled to it. They all had a good laugh at me that night. Including Harlon."

Joe heard Claxton take a sharp breath and knew that if he didn't do something they would all end up in an argument. "All right," he said, "that's enough." His voice was level. "It's been a long day and we're all tired. There's a lot to do tomorrow so we'd better get some sleep. There's no need for any of us to stand guard."

He didn't see any reason to tell them that he thought they'd been watched all afternoon anyway. And if he guessed right, Claxton already knew it, too.

Whether it was induced by fatigue or a full stomach, it really didn't matter, Joe dropped off to sleep almost as soon as his head touched the saddle that he used for a pillow and didn't wake up until he felt a rough hand shaking his shoulder.

"Joe! Joe," Boss Owens's loud voice penetrated his groggy brain. It sounded worried and desperate.

Joe sat up, pushed his hair back and looked up at Boss. Major Claxton was standing by him. His pudgy face was white with pinched lines around his mouth. Joe glanced from one man to the other and knew that something was wrong. Jumping up he looked around and his heart skipped a beat. He didn't see Dorthea Claxton anywhere. Maybe . . .

"She's gone," Claxton said in a tight voice. "Ortez took her in the middle of the night."

"What are you talking about?" Joe asked, tightening the leather thong around his thigh. He thought that for a split second he was still asleep and that Boss and Major Claxton were parties in the same dream.

"He's talkin' about the old gal bein' gone," Boss Owens said, anger in his voice and eyes. He looked more worried than the major did. "Show him the note."

Claxton shot Owens a hateful look but didn't say anything. Instead he handed Joe a piece of yellow paper. Joe took it and looked down at handwriting that he envied. The letters in the short message were perfectly formed and the spelling was correct.

"*Mi compadre*. I have taken your wife, Señora Claxton, to be my guest for a few days. If you do not follow us any farther for the six Gatling guns and go back to the fort I will send her to you by Malito." It was signed simply, "Ortez."

Joe stared down at the paper in his hand. Then he glanced over to where Dorthea Claxton had had her bedroll. It was gone but so was the major's. He looked back up at Edward Claxton. An accusation must have been in Joe's brown eyes.

"We moved our blankets around midnight," Claxton explained, pointing to a cholla tree on the opposite side of the ashes from last night's fire. Both bedrolls were still there. "Maybe we should have stayed on this side." There was only a small amount of remorse in his voice and guilt on his face but not enough to get Joe's sympathy. He wasn't going to tell him that Ortez could have killed them all if he'd wanted to, to make Claxton or himself feel less guilty about Dorthea Claxton's abduction.

"What do you want to do?" Joe asked Claxton, drawing his mouth into a thin line. He already had a good idea what the major's reply would be and he wanted to reach out and choke him. He would be greatly surprised if Claxton's answer was different.

"We're going after the guns," Claxton snapped, glaring Joe straight in the eye, almost daring him to argue with him. "She shouldn't have come along in the first place." He pulled his hat down tightly on his head, turned, walked over and saddled his horse. It was then that Joe realized that the white horse was gone.

Jerking his own bedroll together Joe wondered

why Sarge hadn't made any noise when the Mexicans had taken Dorthea Claxton. The white horse had been hobbled next to Sarge and unless she'd been rendered helpless Dorthea Claxton wouldn't go without a fight. Why didn't she cry out?

Joe realized that he could stand there and ask himself questions until it snowed in this part of the country in July and never get an answer. He only knew that they had to get her back and if they lost the guns, so what?

The three men swung up on their horses and Major Claxton surprised Joe by abruptly heading southeast. They had been heading due south. Why hadn't he changed directions sooner? Once again Joe wondered why Dorthea Claxton had tolerated a man like the major. Then he guessed it was for prestige.

"Their camp is about half a mile ahead," Claxton called out, the first thing he'd said since they'd left the camp.

Joe knew that he, Boss and the major couldn't surprise Ortez and his men if they rode in. They'd have to decide on something else.

When they were about a quarter of a mile from where Claxton said Ortez had his camp, the three men dismounted and started walking. It was soon easy to tell that Claxton wasn't used to doing much walking. He had to stop often, sit down and rest his feet. Joe would have liked nothing better than tie a rope around Claxton and drag him along. What he would really like to do is leave Claxton here and save some time. But they'd need the extra gun. Joe stopped in his tracks when a thought pulled a tight knot in his stomach. What kind of a gun hand was Major Edward Claxton?

When Joe Howard was only a gleam in his father's eye twenty-three years ago, the good Lord must have realized that taking care of him was going to be a full time job and that he would need a lot of help. Joe was about to get a big dose of it.

"I think we should split up," Joe said when they'd stopped for Claxton to rest for the umteenth time.

"I don't think so," Claxton argued, looking quickly from Joe to Boss and back to Joe. "I mean we'll do better if we stay together." He looked scared half to death. "I wish we'd brought O'Connor."

"Maybe we should have," Joe replied resolutely, "but it's too late to think about that now. If we stay together and they spot us," Joe went on, expelling a short breath, "we're finished. If we split up, we could get lucky." He wondered again how Edward Claxton ever became a major.

"I agreed with Joe," Boss said, sending a stream of tobacco juice down between his feet.

"I guess you're right," Claxton gave in, expelling a breath. Taking a pearl handled pistol from the holster, he checked the load and replaced it. Joe got the idea the pistol was used only for show and it had probably never been fired.

Boss Owens checked his own pistol and rifle and turned to the right and started walking. Claxton, with his weapons already checked, took a deep breath, swallowed hard and started walking slowly to the left. That left straight ahead for Joe, or as straight as the winding and narrow trail would allow.

Looking down at the loose sand he felt lucky

indeed when he saw horse tracks, one almost on top of the others. They must have come through here single file, he told himself. There had to have been at least four horses besides Dorthea Claxton's white horse.

He knew Ortez would have lookouts posted and he wasn't disappointed when he eased up an incline and recognized the man standing on an outcropping a little below and to his right. He was one of the riders who'd taken the guns. Joe took off his hat and leaned over farther to see if there were more men. There weren't.

Nerves of indecision ran up and down Joe's back. He couldn't just shoot the man. In his mind that would be murder. A shot would alert Ortez and his men and he might harm Dorthea Claxton. Joe knew he had to get the man closer to him.

Picking up a rock he let it roll down the incline. It served its purpose when it landed a few feet from the Mexican. Joe eased back and tried to flatten himself as much as possible on the ground and still see the bewildered man. He looked around and when he didn't see anything unusual he turned back to his previous position.

He isn't as curious as I'd be, Joe told himself, shaking his head. This time he picked up a handful of pebbles and slid them over the side. That really did the trick. The Mexican looked down, whirled around and looked up in Joe's direction.

I hope he doesn't think it's just an animal and let it go, Joe thought. The Mexican didn't. He turned to his left to begin climbing up the steep incline. Joe was surprised at how fast he could move with a rifle in his hand, a pistol in a holster and two full cartridge belts crossed over his shoulders.

The sun was high up enough now to cast shadows to the west and Joe crouched down behind a boulder just big enough to hide him from the approaching Mexican. Joe could hear the quick steps and knew the Mexican was almost to the top when the steps slowed and he could hear his harsh breathing.

Taking his rifle by the barrel, Joe let the Mexican get almost too close to him before he let him have it across the stomach with the butt. Joe hoped that the unexpected attack would knock the rifle from the Mexican's hand and his wish came true. The Mexican's head snapped back and the big black hat fell off. As the Mexican dropped the rifle, the air swooshed out of his lungs and he made a feeble attempt to draw the long barreled pistol from the holster. Jumping up, Joe raised the rifle up to his shoulder level and brought it down across the Mexican's head with a sickening thud. The brown skinned man didn't utter a sound as his knees buckled under him and he pitched forward.

Joe realized that it wouldn't do any good to try and disguise himself as the lifeless man on the ground. There wasn't time to change into his clothes and besides the Mexican was shorter and thinner. But maybe the hat would give him an edge.

Picking it up and putting it on, Joe wanted to laugh when it fell down around his ears. Looking down at the man on the ground, he soon knew why the hat didn't fit. The man's head was covered with a thick mat of curly black hair. Throwing the hat down on the ground, Joe pick-up his own and replaced it.

Knowing that he was wasting time doing it, but would probably use them later, Joe took the full cartridge belts from around the Mexican's shoulders, dropped them over his own and picked up the rifle. Putting the pistol in his belt he took the few cartridges and put them in his shirt pocket.

Feeling as though he weighed three hundred pounds, Joe took a deep breath and started down the incline that led into a small canyon.

Ortez had planned well if it was his intent to hold Dorthea Claxton in this almost inaccessible place. The walls of the canyon began rising up and it would be hard to pick someone off from the top whereas the person above would have a clear shot at anyone below.

Flattening himself against the jagged wall, Joe eased along all the while looking up. He wondered how Boss Owens and Major Edward Claxton were doing. He hadn't heard any shots which would indicate that either side had gotten anyone. As soon as the thought entered his mind, Joe discarded it. As he'd just proven a few minutes ago, a bullet wasn't the only way to kill someone.

Joe stopped abruptly when he heard voices only a short distance ahead of him. He eased forward and was glad once more that he didn't use spurs. The voices were male and being in Spanish Joe couldn't understand what was being said. He did catch two words: "Señora Claxton" and knew that they were talking about Dorthea Claxton.

Laying the Mexican rifle down, Joe inched forward until he could see the two men. The canyon had opened up with a half circle on the right and desert on the left. The two men were sitting on a log not really paying much attention to the canyon

Joe had just walked through. Then he saw the reason why. A Gatling gun was pointed directly the way he'd come. If he'd been on a horse or making any noise at all the Mexicans would have been alerted and that would have been the end of Joe Howard. Another Gatling gun was aimed up at the rim of the canyon. The other four Gatling guns were aimed out across the desert.

A slight motion to his left caught Joe's eye and he turned his head quickly. Somehow and he would later wonder how he'd done it, Major Edward Claxton was easing along the outer edge of the canyon wall and slowly making his way toward Joe. He was breathing hard. He still had the rifle in his hand. Claxton raised his hand just enough to point upward. Joe stepped away from the wall just enough to see what Claxton was pointing at. Joe raised his head and pulled in a gasp of breath when he saw Boss Owens crawling along the top of the canyon.

When Joe lowered his head and since he'd moved a little he had a wider view inside the canyon. The Mexican leader Ortez was sitting in the shade of a small scrub tree with Dorthea Claxton right at his side. He was saying something to her but they were too far away for Joe to hear. It must have been funny to Ortez because he laughed. Dorthea Claxton, on the other hand wasn't so amused. Her face was immobile.

A fifth Mexican lay on the ground, his hat over his face, not far from a Gatling gun. Joe guessed that was Malito.

Switching his gaze past Ortez and Dorthea Claxton, Joe got a pretty good idea what Ortez had been laughing at. The sixth Mexican was grooming the white horse with a brush. The other six horses were tied under a tree. A cart with huge wooden wheels was standing nearby. Joe wondered if Ortez was planning on taking the white horse for his own. He remembered Ortez riding a Palomino but that horse would never compare to the white.

Joe hated to do it but realized that this was as close as they'd ever come to getting the drop on the six men. But he still wanted to give them half a chance. After all, Ortez could have killed the three of them just as easily as he took the guns yesterday and Dorthea Claxton last night.

Looking over at Claxton, Joe held up three fingers and mouthed the words: "on three" to him. Claxton nodded. Raising his right arm and hoping that Boss could see and understand, he held up three fingers. Boss must have gotten his message because he waved his hand just enough for Joe to see.

Just before Joe gave the signal he glanced back at Claxton and was stunned by what popped into his mind. Claxton didn't care for Joe at all and it wouldn't take but a second for Claxton to turn the rifle on him and his troubles would be over. If Dorthea Claxton and Boss Owens just happened to get killed in the line of fire, he could keep on doing business with Ortez. That was a chance Joe would have to take. The two men stared at each other, one probably knowing what the other was thinking.

As Joe mouthed "on three" to Claxton, he raised his arm and waved to Boss.

"If nobody moves," Joe shouted loud enough for the Mexicans at the back of the canyon to hear, and stepping into everyone's view, "nobody will get hurt." He held the rifle hip level. He knew it was asking a lot but felt better for having done it.

The two Mexicans on the log came alive at the sound of his voice and made a dive for the Gatling gun. The rifle exploded in his hands and the Mexican nearest him grabbed his stomach, screamed in agony, then pitched forward over the log and lay still.

From the corner of his eye Joe saw Major Edward Claxton bring the rifle up to his shoulder and pull the trigger. The second Mexican, taken as much by surprise at his companion's death as Joe's outburst, tried to draw his pistol when he realized that he couldn't reach the Gatling gun. But a bullet from Claxton's rifle caught him in the chest. He grabbed his shirt, pulling at it, then fell over backward.

At the first shot Dorthea Claxon screamed and started to jump up from the ground where she was sitting. But age and Ortez's hand on her arm prevented her doing it. Then as if changing his mind, Ortez jumped up, pulled her roughly to her feet and, drawing his gun, pushed it against her back.

The Mexican at the far end of the canyon with the horses thought he'd have a better chance against Joe and Claxton. He didn't know that Boss Owens was on top of the canyon.

Boss saw Ortez holding the gun on Dorthea Claxton but common sense told him that Ortez wouldn't hurt her. She, in one sense of the word, was his ticket out of here. Instead he shifted his gaze to the Mexican with the horses. He'd leaned down to one side and picked up a rifle. Just as he raised it to his shoulder, Boss squeezed the trigger. He'd never shot anybody in the back before but he knew if he didn't do it, the Mexican would shoot Joe, which he wouldn't like, the major, which he wouldn't mind at all and Dorthea Claxton which he wouldn't allow at all.

Aiming the gun at the Mexican's back, he quickly pulled the trigger and got great satisfaction when the Mexican dropped the rifle and crumpled down by it, a red spot enlarging across his dark blue shirt. At the sound of the rifle and the unexpected movement beside it, the white horse pulled the leather strap loose from the tree and bolted, taking the other horses with it.

While Joe, Ortez, Dorthea Claxton and the major were watching the departing horses, the Mexican lying on the ground decided that now would be a good time to help Ortez. He drew the pistol from the holster, aimed it up at Boss and pulled the trigger. Boss had just stood up when the horses began running and didn't see the Mexican on the ground. The bullet from the .45 caught Boss in the fleshy part of his left shoulder. If he hadn't turned as he stood up, the bullet would have gone right through the center of his chest. Boss swore but nobody heard him, clasped his hand over his shoulder where the blood was already oozing down his arm and dropped to his knees.

Hearing the shot, Joe whirled back around and saw the Mexican standing up and taking another aim at Boss. Slamming a cartridge in the chamber of the rifle, Joe shot the man just as his finger was tightening down on the trigger.

"Joe, look out," Dorthea Claxton's voice was filled with terror as she cried out. "Behind you."

Joe spun around and couldn't believe what he saw. He'd suspected it and thought about it only a little while ago. But he didn't actually believe it would happen. Major Edward Claxton was standing in the same spot as he'd been all along. He was aiming his rifle directly at Joe. The look in his gray eyes was cold and his pudgy features were set. His intent was perfectly clear.

"I don't need you any more, Howard," Claxton said in a level voice. "All I have to do is kill Dorthea after I get through with you. Then Ortez and I can still be in business. I guess Owens is dead up there."

Joe couldn't believe his ears, and he felt sick at his stomach. He'd heard of men plotting against brothers, fathers, and business partners. But never against their wives. He was so stunned by Claxton's plan that he just stared at him. The only thing that brought him out of his stupor was a bullet whizzing past his shoulder from behind.

Joe allowed himself the luxury of a split second glance over his shoulder. Dorthea Claxton's prophesy had come true. She'd just saved his rear end. She was standing, still in front of Ortez. Only this time she held the .32 in both hands.

"Dorthea," Claxton yelled, "put the gun down. Ortez, do something. Shoot her, for God's sake!" Those were the last words Major Edward Claxton would ever speak. The Colt .45 in Joe's holster seemed to leap up into his hand. He was still close enough to Claxton without him having to take direct aim. The gun exploded: Claxton's reflexes made him pull the trigger on the rifle. The rifle went off but the bullet only plowed into the ground in front of Joe's feet. The major dropped the rifle and gripped his chest. For an eon he stared at Joe, hate in his eyes. Then a stain began appearing on his dark coat.

As Dorthea Claxton watched in silence, the man she'd once been so proud of, fell over backward in the sand. For a second his gray eyes looked up at the blue sky then slowly closed.

"Joe, Dorthea, are ye all right?" Boss Owens's wheezy voice asked. He was hurrying down the canyon, holding his shoulder.

"Yeah," Joe nodded, holstering the pistol. Dorthea Claxton was hurrying over to them unmindful that Ortez was still holding his pistol.

"That sorry, low down piece of humanity was going to kill me," she said in a low, bitter voice, putting the pistol back inside her blouse. Unconsciously she reached out and took hold of Boss's right arm. Boss could have died a happy man right then.

"Well, that's all over," Joe said, looking up from the dead man on the ground to his now widow.

"What about him?" Boss asked, pointing over his shoulder toward Ortez who was walking slowly toward them.

"*Sí*, Señor Howard," Ortez replied, a questioning smile on his brown face. "What about me?" He still had the pistol in his hand and could have shot one of them. Or at least Joe.

"None of us has any authority down here," Joe answered, shifting his weight from one foot to the other. "As far as I'm concerned, you still have your guns. The only thing I want you to do is get that white horse back for Mrs. Claxton. She's fought hard to keep it."

Joe and Ortez looked at each other for a long time. A slow smile eased across his brown face and he turned and started walking in the direction the horses had taken.

"It will take a while to bury all of these men," Joe said, touching Dorthea Claxton's arm. "Why don't you go up the canyon and find a shady spot to wait. We'll put the major on a horse and take him back to the fort."

Dorothea Claxton, her head held high now, started walking away but turned around and looked down at the motionless body on the ground. "No," she snapped, a snarl on her mouth. "Bury him here! He doesn't deserve to be buried at the fort." She walked a little farther up the canyon and stopped, turned around and shifted her gaze from Joe to Boss and back to Joe. "If you two are still going to California, I want to go with you."

Joe looked over at Boss. The old man grinned from ear to ear.